If there are consequences of what has just happened, you will tell me.

He'd put stern emphasis on those last words and could still see Serena's face paling beneath his hard gaze. Nikos had spoken in an uncompromising tone, but with his past snapping at his heels, he'd been unable to think rationally, furious that passion had gotten the better of him, making him break his cardinal rule of always being in control. He couldn't blame her for running from him that night. He'd been furious at her—but mostly at himself.

Since the day she'd left, he'd yearned for her, wanted her in his arms at night, but kept firm to the resolute silence that existed between them. As weeks had turned to months, he'd hoped his fears of consequences of their night on the beach were unfounded.

Now, three months after that heated night on the beach, she was back. His heart slammed harder in his chest at the implications of her visit. She may have left it too long to tell him, and almost certainly had ulterior motives, but there was only one reason she was back, and he had to face the fact.

She was carrying his child.

Rachael Thomas

—

From One Night to Wife

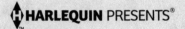
HARLEQUIN PRESENTS®

Recycling programs
for this product may
not exist in your area.

ISBN-13: 978-0-373-13374-1

From One Night to Wife

First North American Publication 2015

Copyright © 2015 by Rachael Thomas

Printed in U.S.A.

Rachael Thomas has always loved reading romance and is thrilled to be a Harlequin Presents author. She lives and works on a farm in Wales, a far cry from the glamour of a Harlequin Presents story, but that makes slipping into her characters' world all the more appealing. When she's not writing or working on the farm, she enjoys photography and visiting historic castles and grand houses. Visit her at rachaelthomas.co.uk.

Books by Rachael Thomas

Harlequin Presents

Craving Her Enemy's Touch
Claimed by the Sheikh
A Deal Before the Altar

Visit the Author Profile page
at Harlequin.com for more titles.

For my brilliantly supportive writing friend Melissa Morgan, who was with me to share those first amazing and exciting moments when my dream of publication came true.

CHAPTER ONE

Nikos Lazaro Petrakis stood and glared out at the sparkling sea beyond the offices of Xanthippe Shipping, his self-built empire, but he didn't see any of it. The words he'd just read in a text burned into his mind. And memories of the only woman who had stirred longings for things he could never allow himself to want set his body alight.

We need to talk. Meet me on the beach tonight. Serena.

Serena James had almost got through his defensive wall, affecting him far more than he cared to admit. He'd been glad when the excuse to banish her from his life had presented itself. He hadn't heard from her since that night three months ago. She'd walked away from him without looking back, rousing memories he'd rather have forgotten, but her silence since had been a welcome relief.

He pressed his eyes shut against the image of Serena. She had been hard to forget and, judging by the way his mind raced now, he still hadn't achieved that aim. For weeks his body had longed for hers. He'd been able to see her, smell her and feel her warmth if he closed his eyes, letting his thoughts slip back. But he'd held firm to his resolution of no commitments. He'd pushed her away emotionally and physically, but hadn't been able to sever the thread of attraction completely. It remained like a web spun in the early dawn, keeping them inextricably linked.

On his return to Athens he'd thrown himself fiercely into his work and had gone after the cruise company Adonia with a ruthlessness that had made even his PA look at him in question.

He clenched his jaw against the heated memories of his time with Serena, knowing there could only be one reason for her return to Santorini, the island he'd grown up on. His eyes snapped open and he inhaled deeply. There could be no other explanation.

During the summer she had arrived on the island to research her next article, and the passionate romance they'd shared had culminated in reckless and unprotected sex on the beach. Were there now life-changing repercussions? Consequences he hadn't planned on and most definitely didn't want?

Alarm bells began to ring. Why had she had waited so long? Had she done as he'd feared and used her journalistic background and connections to find out more about him? Anger fizzed through him as he stared broodily at the view. Did Serena know he wasn't the fisherman he'd led her to believe he was simply because it had been easier that way?

Her job as a travel writer wasn't in the league of working for the national tabloids, but that didn't mean she wouldn't use a story if it presented itself. He'd been extra-careful that she didn't find out who he really was, having had enough of press speculation over his business dealings, as well as over his constant succession of female companions.

If he'd known Serena's profession before their first amazing night together he might have been able to walk away, instead of being snared by her innocence and drawn in too deep towards something he'd always resisted.

To his sceptical mind there was only one reason she was here on the island, demanding to see him instead of simply calling. After believing she was different from all the other women he'd dated, she'd proved him wrong. She was here to use his wealth in order to secure her future and it couldn't have come at a worse time. His deal for Adonia Cruise Liners could be lost if her story got out.

He swore aggressively, but the words did not ease the suspicion that filled him. Irritated, he marched from the windows to his desk, stabbing at the buttons on the phone. The calm enquiry of his PA cut through the rage of his emotions and he forced them back under control. How could Serena ruffle his equanimity so spectacularly even when she wasn't in his company?

'Organise my plane. I need to go to Santorini this afternoon.'

The Greek words were fluid and assertive as control flooded through him once more, but his anger towards Serena and the situation didn't abate. Suspicion surfaced again. Why had she chosen now to come back? What did she want?

Did she know he was in the final and delicate negotiation stages of acquiring a cruise company? Expanding his shipping beyond freight and into the world of luxury cruises? It would make him CEO of the biggest shipping company in Greece. He didn't need the added complications she might bring with her. Not now—not ever.

Despite the looming deal, his mind was drawn to back to Serena: vivacious, happy and utterly gorgeous. She'd made him want things he couldn't have. The fact that no other man had ever made love to her—that she'd given *him* her virginity—had complicated the issue, and he'd forced himself to say goodbye, turning his back on what they'd briefly shared. Because of his past it was impossible to make an emotional commitment—even if he wanted to. Never again would he be that vulnerable.

Nikos took a deep breath and strode to the window, watching as a large cruise liner docked with an ease belying its size. Beyond that several container ships waited on the horizon, but the familiar sense of fulfilment from seeing the reality of his hard work and dreams out at sea didn't come. Nothing before had ever taken the edge off standing at his window and looking at all he'd achieved, but right now his mind was elsewhere, unable to focus on anything other than the memory of the slender redhead who for two weeks had driven him wild with desire.

He could still see her pale face, and the green eyes that had always sparkled with life like the sea beneath the dazzling sun. Her silky hair, as red as autumn leaves, had begged his fingers to slide through it. Each smile had invited his kisses so tantalisingly.

The last words he'd said to her forged forward in his memory—as did the image of her standing on the beach, dusting sand from her clothes, her face flushed from the passion that had engulfed them so spectacularly that evening. He should have had more control, more restraint, but she'd made that impossible. Just holding her in his arms, feeling her curves against his body and her soft lips beneath his, had been too much temptation.

Had that been what she'd intended? He balled his hands into tight fists of frustration, hearing again his words that night, harsh and unyielding, breathing life into the worst scenario as he'd made his position clear.

'If there are consequences of what has just happened you will *tell me.'*

He'd put stern emphasis on those last words and could

still see her face paling beneath his hard gaze. As she'd looked up at him the desire burning in her eyes had slipped away faster than the setting sun. He'd spoken in a stern and uncompromising tone, but with his past snapping at his heels he'd been unable to think rationally, furious that passion had got the better of him, making him break his cardinal rule of always being in control.

He couldn't blame her for running from him that night. He'd been furious at her—but mostly at himself.

Since the day she'd left he'd yearned for her, wanted her in his arms at night, but he had held firm to the resolute silence that had existed between them. As weeks had turned to months he'd hoped his fear of consequences of their night on the beach was unfounded.

Now, three months after that heated night under the stars, she was back. His heart slammed harder in his chest at the implications of her visit. She might have left it too long to tell him, and almost certainly had ulterior motives, but there was only one reason she was back and he had to face the fact.

She was carrying his child.

Serena's heart thumped hard as she waited on the beach, with the day ebbing faster than the tide. Where was Nikos? Would he come?

The rhythmic rush of the waves over the sand did little to calm her.

During her flight from London thoughts of the amazing two weeks they'd spent together had been overshadowed by her accidental discovery of Nikos's true identity only minutes before she'd boarded the plane. The man she'd fallen in love with was far from the humble fisherman he'd described himself as being all those months ago. She'd been sitting in the departure lounge and Nikos's image had flashed across the news app on her phone, with a story speculating on the Greek shipping billionaire's involvement in an aggressive takeover bid.

Nikos was a shipping billionaire?

She'd chosen to fly out to Santorini believing that he had very little money, but that he at least deserved to be given her news in person. Her shocking discovery, moments before she'd boarded her flight, had changed everything. Angry and betrayed, all she wanted now was to upset Nikos's profitable little world and turn it upside down—just as he'd done hers.

As she stood on the beach the bravado she'd built up during the flight threatened to desert her. He would know exactly why she was here, but it didn't make what she had to tell him any easier—whoever he was. He didn't want 'consequences', as he had so nicely put it, and of that she was certain.

The tiny stirrings of hope she'd allowed to grow…that they might have a future together…had been crushed completely. A man like Nikos—a billionaire—would most certainly wash his hands of her.

Instinctively she placed her palm protectively over her stomach and the new life within. What if Nikos didn't come? She'd wanted him to acknowledge that their passionate holiday affair had resulted in pregnancy. Now she wasn't so sure. Did she want a man like that in her life? In her child's life?

How *could* he have deceived her? She despised liars, having lived in the shadow of lies all her life.

She scoured her memory for that last night on the island. The gentle, loving fisherman she'd fallen in love with had changed drastically, showing a new and unfamiliar side, when he'd realised what might come of their spontaneous lovemaking.

It should have been just a goodbye kiss—one she could keep in her memory when she'd returned to her life in England. She'd known he didn't want more, and had accepted it, wanting to experience love for the first time in the arms of a man who demanded nothing—the man she loved. But they'd both lost control as passion had claimed them, neither caring about anything other than the desire that had raged between them like wildfire, engulfing everything in its path.

A flurry of panic rose up again. She hadn't told anyone yet—not even her family. She couldn't bear to see their reactions, knowing she'd let them down. Her sister knew of her brief romance with Nikos, but she hadn't found the courage to tell her about the baby—not now, with all of Sally's IVF problems.

'Serena.'

She closed her eyes as she heard his voice behind her, deep and heavily accented. She couldn't turn yet. The wretchedness she felt would surely be in her eyes. Either that or her love for him might still shine through, and that was something she just couldn't let him see. Not after the way he'd cut her out of his life because of a mistake in the making, made by both of them.

A *mistake*. She hated that word. She'd lived with it hanging over her all her life. She was one of those—a mistake that had taken her parents by surprise. Forcing them to reconcile their differences and remain married.

'Serena,' he said again, and touched her arm.

She couldn't avoid the moment any longer. Her breath caught in her throat and somersaulting butterflies took flight in her stomach.

She was more nervous than she'd ever been in her life as she turned to face him, desperate to keep her voice calm. 'I had almost given up on you.'

Was that wobbly whisper really her voice? She must stay strong. Her unbalanced emotions couldn't get the better of her—not now. But as she moved back from his touch she questioned if she could go through with this. Was she doing the right thing? Should she even have come here?

Nikos moved closer to her, forcing her to look up at him, and when she did she could hardly suppress a gasp of surprise. His blue eyes, so uncharacteristic for a Greek man, weren't the colour of a summer sky, as she remembered them, but icy cold. He'd changed. This was a very different man from the one she'd fallen in love with. And it wasn't only the smart clothes he now wore instead of the tatty work jeans she'd always seen him in.

He was still tall, dark haired, with angled features, but each angle looked harsher, and his lips were set in a don't-mess-with-me line of rigidness.

'Sorry I had business to attend to.'

'You look...' She paused as she struggled to find the right word, completely taken aback by his unyielding aura. His deceit, and the enormity of what she was about to announce made small talk almost impossible. The next few minutes would affect the rest of her life and she almost faltered, but bravely pushed on. 'You look very smart— very much the businessman.'

His brows lifted in surprise and she thought she saw a hint of anger in the blue depths of his eyes. There was hardly a trace of the man she'd laughed and loved with for the duration of her holiday three months ago—the man she had given much more than just her heart to. This was the real Nikos.

'I may have been brought up a simple fisherman, but that doesn't mean I have to stay that way.'

The sharpness of his words made her blink, and again she took a step backwards, the sand shifting beneath her feet. She glanced around the now deserted beach in a desperate attempt to avoid that stern glare.

He wasn't making it easy for her. It was obvious from his irritation that he knew why she was here—why she'd sought him out after he'd so cruelly ended their two weeks of romance. He was toying with her, forcing her to tell him.

'Do you know why I'm here?'

She hated the way her words trembled, and resisted the urge to hug her arms about herself in an attempt to protect herself from his anger. Whatever else she did, she had to remain strong.

He didn't take his gaze from her face. She stood firm, refusing to be intimidated as his cold words rose above the rush of the waves.

'You should have done this about two months ago.'

Each matter-of-fact word lacerated her heart, almost annihilating the love for him she'd carried in her heart since she'd left the island. Each carefully spoken word proved she had been nothing more than a convenient amusement.

Whatever her dreams of Nikos had been, to him she'd only been a passing fancy—a brief encounter that didn't require commitment, just soft words and passionate kisses. One he thought he could brush aside when it suited him. But things had changed and now he had to acknowledge the situation.

Enraged by his attitude, and all she'd learnt, she faced up to him, the fire of determination scorching through her. 'For the past two and a half months I have been somewhat preoccupied with nausea.'

Each sharp word flew at him like a dagger. The injustice of his accusation was stinging, giving her the strength to stand her ground. After desperately keeping her pregnancy from her family, the strain was too much. He was pushing her almost to breaking point.

'You could have called. I did, after all, ask to be told.'

His blue eyes had become so dark and forbidding they were like the hidden depths of the ocean. Unknown and uninviting.

'Ask?' The word rushed from her, wrapped tightly in disbelief. 'You didn't *ask* anything. You *demanded*.'

His eyes hardened, glinting like icicles as the full moon shone on them and fixed her to the spot. 'I was doing the right thing. I asked that you tell me if you became pregnant. I did not demand anything of you. It would only have taken one call, Serena. Why wait so long? Why now?'

'I needed time to think—to decide what I was going to do.' She'd thought herself into circles. Total panic had made any kind of sensible thought impossible, but even then the answer had been the same.

Nikos had no intention of being a father. She would have to bring up her child alone. Such thoughts had driven her mad with fear and panic, as had the conviction that her mother would be devastated. Her daughter falling pregnant after little more than a one-night stand would be too much of a nightmare for her to deal with. And she wasn't a naive teenager, which would only make her mother's reaction worse. She always worried about what other people thought of her—that was why she'd hidden the sham of her marriage behind a facade of happiness.

At twenty-three Serena should have known better. But, having purposely kept any advances at arm's length, she hadn't.

The experience of making love with a man was something she'd planned to share with someone she loved. So when Nikos had sauntered into her life, sweeping her off her feet, she'd known almost from the moment they'd met where it would end. She'd given Nikos, the man she'd fallen instantly in love with, her most precious gift.

In doing so she'd let everyone down. But worse to bear was the pain she would cause her sister.

'To decide what you were going to do?'

She saw his brows quirk together savagely as his gruff voice startled her out of her thoughts.

'Yes—*do*.' He was beginning to exasperate her. He was making her do all the work in this conversation, forcing every word from her when he didn't even have the decency to admit his deceit. Was it a form of punishment?

'And have you thought?'

The powerful aura radiating from him was something she hadn't noticed before, even though they'd spent almost every evening of her time on the island together. Not only did he look different, he acted differently. This Nikos was totally in command, completely intimidating—and, worse than anything else, he was without care or kindness.

She met it head-on with a cold indifference that hid the panic and nerves she really felt.

'Yes, I've thought, Nikos. I've thought of your lies, and of those callous words you threw at me the last time I saw you. I've thought of nothing other than your insistence that I inform you of any *consequences*.'

His mouth was set in a grim line of irritation, but she pushed on. Behind him the sky displayed beautiful oranges and deep purples, and she wondered how such a stunning sunset could play host to this terrible moment.

'It seems I'm now to be punished for not telling you as soon as I knew, but—more fool me—I wanted to tell you personally. Face-to-face. Not in a phone call. And that meant waiting until now—until I felt well enough to travel.'

'Yet you can't.' He moved closer, his words coming out in a provoking growl. 'You can't say it, can you?'

'Oh, I can, Nikos—I *can*.' Fury charged through her

like a tornado. Her heart raced and each breath she took became deeper. He was killing her love, shattering any hope she had harboured. Despite the turmoil her mind was in, the irrational sway of emotions, she flung the words he wanted to hear forcefully at him. 'I'm *pregnant*, Nikos. I'm pregnant with your child.'

'Why have you come all this way, Serena? What exactly do you want from me?'

He stepped closer, towering over her, intimidating. She hated the way her breath caught in her throat, hated the way her body longed for his even as his icy words splintered around her.

'I don't want anything from you. At least not from Nikos the fisherman—but that isn't you, is it?' She lifted her chin, aiming for defiance—which was far from the uncertainty she was fighting so hard to conceal.

His eyes narrowed and he pierced her with a fierce stare. 'How much?'

Serena's mind swam with confusion. What was he talking about? 'How much what?'

She backed away, unable to deal with the close proximity of his body. How had she ever thought coming to the island was a good idea? She'd wanted to tell him face-to-face to convince herself that any hope of more was futile, knowing it would be the only way to prevent that *what if* feeling.

'Money.'

He spat the word at her so venomously she stepped back even further, until the backs of her legs met the large rock she'd been sitting on whilst waiting for him. She'd never thought telling him would be easy, but this was totally unexpected. Did he think she was here just for financial gain?

'I don't want your money.' Her head began to swim and

giddiness threatened, but she couldn't stop now. Not until she'd told him everything. 'All I wanted to do was tell you in person and leave.'

She looked up at him, wishing things were different— that he hadn't lied, that he hadn't said the words that still replayed over and over in her mind. *'You will tell me.'* The insistent way he'd delivered them had left her in no doubt that fathering a child was the last thing he wanted.

She took in a deep and silent breath and thought of her sister, and the heartbreak she and her husband had been through each time IVF had failed. It seemed so unfair to find out that she'd become pregnant so easily when her sister was breaking her heart, wanting a child. It was just too cruel, and it had left her unable to say anything to her family, let alone confide in her sister. The only person she'd told was Nikos. And right now he was making her feel alone and isolated.

Her time with Nikos had been nothing more than a holiday romance—one of many for him, she was sure. But for her it had changed everything—for ever—and he'd just confirmed her worst fear. He was going to turn his back on her *and* his child.

She briefly closed her eyes against the torrent of emotions that coursed through her. Pain induced by Nikos, infused with the ever-present hurt of knowing she'd been an unexpected addition to her family, forcing her parents to stay together. If only Nikos felt something for her everything might be different, but that was evidently a hopeless dream. She should walk away now—for her baby's sake, if not hers.

'You think you can tell me I am about to be a father and then just leave?'

He moved away from her, towards the ebbing tide, and turned to look out at the sea. His broad shoulders were tense, but she was glad she wasn't under his scrutiny any longer.

I don't know what to do. The words screamed inside her head as intense pain stabbed at her heart. She pressed the pads of her fingers to her closed eyes. Going down that line of thought now wouldn't accomplish anything.

Guilt boiled inside her—as if she'd stolen something from her sister. Especially as she knew there wouldn't be any more IVF for her after the last treatment. Her sister and her husband didn't have any savings left.

'How can we raise a child, Nikos?'

Her words were a tremulous whisper as she moved to stand beside him. The rush of the waves suddenly sounded loud on the beach as she looked at his profile. Not for the first time, she wondered who this man was.

Images of the handsome man she'd had an affair with filled her mind as she looked away and out across the sea. The setting sun was almost gone from the sky. But she didn't see its beauty. All she saw was Nikos, the man she'd given her heart to, believing she loved him and that he might love her. During those long, hot days his dark hair had gleamed beneath the sun and his blue eyes had filled with desire each time they'd met.

He had been everything she'd ever dreamed of and more, sweeping her away so fast she'd given up her teenage dreams of waiting to find her true love before discovering the pleasure of intimacy with a man. She didn't regret one moment of that decision. She'd loved Nikos—until he'd looked at her with his condemning eyes on that last night.

He didn't respond and instinctively she reached out to him, touching his arm. As he turned and looked at her she saw his face wore an expression of pain, and she had the unexpected urge to throw herself into his arms, to be held tight and told everything was going to be okay. Because deep down it was what she wanted—what she needed. To be loved by only this man. But the man she loved didn't exist.

Instead she stood as tall and proud as possible, finding strength she hadn't realised she had left. 'We can't, Nikos. Not together.'

'What are you saying, Serena?' Nikos all but stumbled over his words as the implications of what she'd said almost silenced him. The reality of the situation had hit him hard, taking away the ability to speak.

Memories of the day his mother had left and questions from his past rushed forward. He tried hard to prevent them from colliding with the present, but he couldn't shake them off. His father had cursed her, saying he should never have married an English girl, and Nikos had stood alone, ignored and forgotten by each of them. Then his mother had left, her cruel parting words ringing in his ears.

If his father had still been alive he could have found out more about the mother he barely remembered. As a teenager he'd been angry when he'd learnt that her career had been more important than her marriage and her young son. So when she'd made contact on his sixteenth birthday, saying she'd never meant to hurt him, he'd blocked her from his life. He didn't want to open that door again.

He clenched his hands into tight fists. Fury carried through the years raged inside him, but he pushed it back. He had to keep calm.

That letter from his mother had made him vow never to marry. He had no intention of making the same mistake as his parents. But that vow also denied him the possibility of being a father.

Something shifted inside him. *Serena was carrying his child.* He took in a deep, steadying breath. He was going to be a father. Fate had altered his life decision and no matter what Serena did or said he would be a father to his child in every way. His past would not write his child's future. His child would not experience the heartache he'd known and he'd do everything in his power to achieve that.

'Neither of us can give this child what it needs.'

Her voice was soft, with a definite and unyielding firmness. He looked down at her, hardly able to believe what he was hearing. He couldn't comprehend the cool and composed words that had slipped easily from her mouth. She was writing off her child as easily as his mother had done.

An icy-cold chill slipped down his spine and the image of the woman before him combined with that of the fair-haired woman in the tatty photograph he'd kept hidden away since he'd been given it by his grandmother. It was his mother—but as far as he was concerned it was just the woman who'd given birth to him. He'd locked it away, out of sight and out of mind, hating her too much to acknowledge her as his mother.

Serena blinked rapidly and he thought he saw a glimmer of moisture, the smallest hint of tears. He narrowed his eyes, assessing the situation. His breath, deep and hard, almost burned his chest as his heart was pumped full of anger, his mouth filled with the bitter taste of betrayal as he remembered what had sounded like a throwaway comment at the time.

Had she planned this from the very start? She'd seduced him so wickedly with her kisses that last night on the beach that he'd lost all control. Had that been her intention all along?

He furrowed his brow, resisting the need to put distance between them. She'd been a virgin the first time they'd made love, which had shocked him so much that he'd fallen under her spell, wanting to spend more and more time with her, yet unable to allow himself to want her emotionally. Had he been naive to be seduced by her?

'I never planned to be a father, but that doesn't mean I won't be there for my child.'

He clenched his fists against the fear of what those words meant. Could he really be a good father when his own had ignored him so much that his grandparents had been compelled to taken him in?

'I will.'

A spark of something akin to fear mingled with hope showed in her eyes as she moved closer. 'You want to raise the baby with me?'

He shut his heart to the image of a happy family, slamming the door firmly. 'That won't be possible, will it? Not if you have already decided to give it away like a parcel.'

'I haven't decided any such thing.' She glared at him like a wounded animal, wary and untrusting.

'You constantly spoke of your sister—about her longing for a baby. Do you recall what you told me?' The harsh words growled from him, and before she could reply he pressed on. '"*If I could have a baby for her, I would.*" Those were your exact words.'

'How can you twist things like that? It's what I wished I could do—not what I planned.'

Disappointment rushed over him like a waterfall. When she'd asked if he wanted to raise the baby with her he'd almost allowed himself to believe it was what she wanted, that it could be possible. How foolish.

'Did you really think you could come here and use the baby—my baby—as a bargaining tool to get money for your sister? Or, worse, give my baby to her?'

She pushed slim fingers through the thickness of her red hair, distracting him momentarily.

'No. That's not how it is. This is *my* baby.'

'It's my baby too, Serena.' Fury thundered in his veins, pulsing around him so fast he couldn't think straight. It was obvious she'd done her homework. She knew who he was. But was she really capable of seducing him, hoping to become pregnant with a baby for her sister? If he was thinking rationally he'd say no, but with such a revelation knocking him sideways he'd believe anything right now.

As she stood there, glaring angrily at him, challenging him on every level, he knew he had to be there for his baby as it grew up. He wanted to give it all he'd never had. But it didn't matter how much money he had, he didn't know if he could do the one thing a father should. Love his child—or anyone.

How could he when he'd never known the love of his parents? And he'd always kept his distance from his grandparents, shunned their love, preferring to stay safe behind his defences even as a young boy. But he had a bond with them. Could he at least bond with his child?

Was he heartless? Was that why his mother had turned her back on him? Why his father had barely looked at him? Was it his fault?

'I will be there for my child.' He watched her for a hint of guilt, any trace of her deceit.

'What's *that* supposed to mean?'

The fury in her voice overflowed, confirming his suspicions.

'Drop the innocent act. You know who I am. For a woman with your journalist's training it must have been all too easy to discover more about the father or your child.' Venom spiked every word as he looked at her, suddenly becoming aware of the waves creeping closer to them. How long had they been discussing this? Hours? Seconds? He didn't know. Only that it would change things and change *him* for ever.

'I have only just looked you up on the internet—in the departure lounge at the airport, to be exact. Because, stupidly, I believed you were an island fisherman, living a simple life. There shouldn't have been anything more to know.' Her furious words were flung at him and her eyes sparked like fireworks. 'You lied to me, used me.'

So the flame-haired temptress had a temper!

'Just as you lied to *me*—using me, the "simple fisherman", as a means to an end.'

'I didn't use you at all.'

'So you *deny* you seduced me in the hope of getting pregnant with a child you planned to give to your sister?'

She gasped in shock, her acting skills well and truly on display. 'Of *course* I do.'

'In that case I won't be upsetting your plans.'

'And what does *that* mean?'

Her temper flared again. Begrudgingly he admired her spirit. She was even more beautiful when the fire of determination rose up within her.

'Only that I have every possible means at my disposal and I *will* be a father to my child, no matter what obstacles you put in my way. I will remove each and every one to get what I want. My child. My heir.'

CHAPTER TWO

SERENA WAS SPEECHLESS. She blinked rapidly as if seeing Nikos for the first time. What did he mean? Her head began to swim as she tried to process what he was saying and she cursed her pregnancy-induced emotions, biting back hard against the urge to dissolve into frustrated tears.

This wasn't going at all to plan. She hadn't expected him to welcome her with open arms—not after his parting words—but the discovery of his deceit and his determination to overrule her was totally unexpected.

'You let me think you were an island fisherman. One who shouldn't have anything more to tell.'

She'd known coming back to Santorini wouldn't give her all she really wanted, but never in all her wildest dreams had she imagined this scenario.

She looked at Nikos again, searching for the man she'd fallen in love with. The man who'd set light to the undiscovered woman inside her, capturing her heart and body.

'Why?' she asked simply.

'It was for the best at the time.' Each word was firm and decisive, his face a mask of composure.

I will remove each and every one to get what I want. My child. My heir.

His words of warning echoed in her head like a haunting melody. It seemed that no matter how much she'd tried to be different from her parents, wanting only to have a happy family, she was heading down the same path.

Her parents had been forced to stay together by an unplanned pregnancy, a mistake. She had grown up carrying the guilt of being that mistake, knowing she had forced her parents to stay together. *She* was the reason they'd fought, the reason they hated each other now. She didn't want her child to suffer the same guilt because of the mistake she and Nikos had made.

'I *am* an island fisherman.'

He stepped towards her, his voice softer now, but instinct told her not to let her guard drop, that trouble was brewing.

'But I am also a businessman. My office is in Piraeus and I live in Athens.'

'So what were you doing on the island? Using the guise of a fisherman to lure women and bolster your ego?' She couldn't stop the words from rushing at him.

He glared at her. 'Fishing was my grandfather's trade, his business. I help out with the fleet that he started. And knowing your background I wasn't going to disclose anything personal to you.'

'My background?' She was completely at a loss as to what he meant.

'You *are* a journalist, are you not?'

She tried hard to process what he was telling her, but couldn't understand why he'd kept the truth from her. Was it really because she had studied journalism? Did he really fear that? Or was it simply that he hadn't wanted her to know who he was?

'Why did you feel the need to hide it from me, Nikos?' She couldn't imagine the life Nikos really led. It was too far removed from the man she'd met, the man she'd fallen in love with. He was shattering every dream she'd had of him. 'Why were you even here, masquerading as a fisherman?'

'My life changed when I left the island, and my fortunes with it.' He looked at her, his eyes glacial and hard, his expression unyielding. 'Every year since, I've spent two weeks helping the small fleet of fisherman here on the island. It's a way of staying connected to my grandparents. And you didn't ask questions—which made a change.'

'A change from what?' He wasn't making sense—or was it her jumbled emotions? She was tired. Thinking coherently wasn't easy, but she forced her mind to concentrate.

'From women wanting all they can get from me—financially and emotionally. It appears you are not different after all.'

'You lied—you hid the truth—because you were afraid I'd want more?' The words rushed from her before she could hold them back and his eyes narrowed in response, his mouth setting into an irritated line of hardness.

The stark question he'd fired at her earlier came back, its full meaning now painfully clear.

'How much?'

That was what he'd said when she'd told him she only wanted one thing from him. It hadn't made any sense. Now it hit her. He thought she wanted money from him—or worse still, that she'd deliberately got pregnant to give the baby to Sally.

Sickness rose up and her head spun. What kind of man was he?

'Why didn't you tell me when we were together?' She hurled the question at him, her knees becoming ever weaker with shock as nausea threatened to take over.

'What we shared…' He took her hands in his and she hated the way her pulse leapt at his touch, counteracting all the pain and turmoil of moments before. 'It was something special. But it was never destined to be more than a holiday romance, a passing affair.'

He was right about that, at least. She had wished and hoped for more, but deep down had known it would finish once she'd left the island and returned to her life. What she *hadn't* known was that he too would leave the island and go back to his life. A life he'd kept from her because he'd believed she was after his money or the scoop of a big story.

She pulled her hands from his slowly and shook her head in despair. 'It doesn't mean we can raise a child together, Nikos. Money isn't everything.'

Fury seeped through Nikos's veins like poison, mixing with memories of the day his mother had walked away and left him. Serena's words, although calmly said, screamed inside his head. What was she saying? What plans had she been making for their child whilst he'd been living in ignorance of its existence?

'It still sounds very much as if you are considering giving my baby away.' Incredulity made his tone sharper than a blade.

'That is absurd.'

She met his accusation head-on, looking determined to do battle and defend herself. And he knew for certain that there could only be one reason. He'd exposed her plans before she'd had a chance to knock him sideways with the idea, but all it had done was make him ever more certain that he would be there for his child—not just now and again, but all the time.

'You have more than implied it.'

He clenched his hands into tight fists, resisting the need to reach for her, to hold her arms and force her to look him in the eye and tell him the truth.

'We can't sort this out now—not when you are jump-
ing to such outrageous conclusions.'

She looked at him tempestuously and her green eyes
met his, but his usual accuracy in reading a person had
deserted him. He couldn't see lies or truth, but he did see
something else in them. The same fiery passion he'd seen
three months ago—which had been his undoing.

He stepped closer to her…so close he could smell the
sweetness of her perfume. He battled with his memories
of their time together as the scent of summer flowers invaded his senses, light and floral, evoking more memories he'd do better to bury. But he couldn't. This woman,
the only one who'd made him want more than a brief affair, was in reality no better than his mother. Worse, in
fact. She wanted to abandon her child, and she expected
him to do the same.

'Nikos, we have to be practical. The baby will grow up
in England—with me.'

Never. The word resounded in his head. *Never.*

He ignored the pleading edge to her voice, wondering
if she thought he'd meekly accept that. Would she really
be a mother to his child? Or had she planned all along to
give her baby away?

His thoughts returned to his mother with unnerving
clarity. Had she been being practical when she'd walked
away? Had she given her six-year-old son a thought as she'd
left, preferring to escape with her lover, to the bright city
lights and her modelling career, instead of remaining on
the island with the man she'd married?

Nikos tried to push back the demons that had haunted
him since that day. The woman who'd given birth to him
didn't know him—just as he didn't know her. He might
have passed her on the streets of Athens, or any other city
he'd visited for business, and not known. All he knew was

that despite her attempts to contact him since he'd turned sixteen he'd written her out of his life.

He looked at Serena, the woman he might have loved if things had been different—if his past hadn't convinced him he was incapable of love or being loved.

'No.'

The word was fired harshly from him like a bullet and, precisely aimed, it found its mark. Serena's eyes widened in surprise and those long lashes blinked rapidly in confusion. Did she *have* to be so beautiful? So compelling even in the heat of this war she'd waged?

'You can't just say no. We haven't sorted anything.'

She looked beseechingly up at him, searching his face, and he took a deep breath as memories of kissing those soft lips avalanched over him. Did she know the effect she was having on him? Did she realise that right at this moment he couldn't think past what they'd had, those passionate moments they'd shared in the summer?

The waves rushed to the shore with a normality that stunned him. Apparently they were not aware of the horrendous situation unfolding on the sand. The lights of the small town glowed like stars around them and he found his past colliding with the present, becoming inseparable.

'How can I trust you not to abandon my child to your sister after what you said?'

His voice was an angry growl, and he fought hard against the rage of emotions that forged through him. All his life he'd carried the hurt of total rejection by the one woman who should have loved him unconditionally.

'I'm not abandoning my child to anyone—not even to you.'

For a moment he thought he saw pain flash in her eyes, thought he saw the agony of it on her face, but it was gone in an instant. Hard lines of determination replaced it.

'Telling me we can't raise this child together after saying your sister is desperate for a baby sounds very much like you are planning just that.'

He moved back from her, not trusting the rage that had become like the rush of a river in flood. All the childhood doubts he'd successfully locked away were now out and running riot.

'How can you even think of doing such a thing?'

'How can you even think *that*?' She gasped out the pained words. 'I want this child. I want to give it everything I possibly can.'

The conviction in her voice struck a raw nerve. 'As do I.'

'Can you really give our child all it needs when you admit you don't want to be a father?'

She moved towards him, her hand momentarily reaching out to him, but he flinched from her touch, his raw emotions making coherent thought difficult.

How could she doubt he would give his child all it needed? The idea of being a father was one that he had always savagely dismissed because it would entail marriage—something he'd proved he'd be unable to commit to—but now he was presented with the reality he knew exactly what he wanted.

'A child needs love.'

Vehemently the words rushed from him, and he was annoyed at her ability to take away his composure, his control. He knew more than most that a child needed love. It was all he'd craved as a young boy. But could he be a father? Could he love his child? His father hadn't been able to and his mother never had. She'd admitted that as she'd left. How could he be any different from them?

Serena laughed—a soft, nervous laugh, but a laugh nonetheless. He bit down hard, clenching his teeth, trying to stop harsh words rushing out.

'Can you really do that, Nikos?'

His silence seemed to answer her question and she ploughed on with her own arguments for being a single parent.

'Can you love a child you don't want?'

'Do not question my ability to be a father,' he growled, hardly able to contain his anger.

'A child needs stability, a loving home. It doesn't matter if it's with one parent or two, so long as it has all it needs.'

Strength sounded in her voice and her face was full of determination as she looked into his eyes, challenging him with everything she had.

'I've already made it clear that is not a problem.' He knew his voice had turned to a low growl, full of anger, but her constant referral to his inability to provide for his child was more than he could take.

'It's your deceit, Nikos, that has made me think you can't.' Her face was stern as she looked at him. 'Your lies haven't changed anything just as your real identity hasn't. I will not allow my baby to become a possession to be bargained over. Least of all by you.'

'After your scheme to get pregnant you are not in a position to make demands on me.'

He felt the reins of control slipping, felt her gaining the moral high ground—especially now haunting images from his childhood were being rapidly unleashed.

'That is *so* far from the truth,' she retaliated hotly, then moved towards him, her voice softening. 'This wasn't planned, at all, and I cannot even *consider* giving away my baby.'

Suddenly he was a young boy again, standing on this very beach, looking out to sea, hoping the next boat that came in would have his mother on board, that she would change her mind and come home. He'd watched and waited for many years, before finally dismissing her from his mind, his thoughts and his heart. She was a cold and heartless woman and he'd accepted the fact that he'd never see her again.

'But you want money?'

'Nikos, this isn't about money. I believed you couldn't afford to raise a child—just as I can't. It doesn't mean I'm not going to try, though. I hadn't planned on having a child, but I am certainly going to be there for him or her—all the time.'

Him or her. Suddenly the child she carried had gained an identity, an image in his mind. It would either be a little girl, with flame-red hair like her mother's, or a little boy with a cheeky smile and plenty of attitude.

Then her words sank into his mind. Had she really thought he couldn't afford to raise his child? The niggling suspicion that she'd known who he really was resurfaced. It wouldn't have been hard for her to source information about him on the internet. His business acumen made him a much talked of man—as did his single status. He didn't believe she'd only just found out.

She reached out for him again and he resisted the urge to draw back, strangely wanting to feel the heat of her touch.

'I am having this baby, Nikos. With or without you.'

He snapped back his arm, suddenly not wanting to be touched by her after all, not wanting the hot sizzle that sparked through him to take over.

That was one thing he had to control: he couldn't desire her.

Serena's heart sank as he pulled away from her. He hated her touch, and the anger in his eyes worried her. Whatever else had gone before, and whatever was to come, they had created a new life together. They had to find a way to give their baby the best. Which meant agreeing on how that was to be done.

Images unwittingly filled her mind. Nikos at her side as she held a baby, its hair as dark as his and with the same deep blue eyes looking up at her.

The image of happiness ripped her heart in two. That kind of happy-ever-after was what she'd wished for herself as a child. She'd wanted nothing more than for her parents to be happy together, and most of all she wished they'd wanted her, their youngest child. Instead she'd had to face the reality that she'd been a sudden and unexpected addition to the family—one that had put pressure on the cracks that had already been showing between her parents.

'Where do you propose the baby grows up?' Nikos moved closer, his barely concealed annoyance clearly evident.

'With *me*.' Desperation echoed in every word and she saw him inhale deeply, holding on to the anger her words had provoked.

'In England?'

The syllables of his words were broken, the sound staccato and harsh. She swallowed as she looked at him—anything else would show a weakness, one he'd exploit fully.

'Yes.'

Serena thought of all the heartache her sister had endured, the number of times she'd hoped for a baby and the number of times her dreams had come crashing down. She had indeed discussed it with Nikos, and couldn't believe he was now using it against her.

It was a really cruel twist of fate that it was *her* who'd fallen pregnant—and from just one night of unprotected sex. But it had been more than that—for her at least. That last evening on the secluded beach they'd walked hand in hand as the sun had set and shared a gentle kiss. It had rekindled the fire of passion they'd experienced in her small hotel room.

She reminded herself that from the outset Nikos had made it clear he didn't consider theirs a lasting romance, but one that would end when she went home. She'd gone along with the idea, feeling secure in the knowledge that she could walk away, that it didn't have to be more. But she'd fallen hopelessly in love with Nikos.

That night, as they'd reached the seclusion of the edge of the beach, surrounded by rocks and caves, he'd kissed her so passionately they hadn't been able to stop. The urgency of their desire had forced them down onto the cool sand, but nothing had prepared her for his reaction afterwards—those cold words of dismissal, the demand that he should know if 'consequences' resulted. Well, they had.

'So *you* would see our child grow up, hear its first words, watch its first steps, while I would be relegated to the background, lucky to catch a glimpse of it before it becomes a teenager?'

His voice brought her rapidly back to the present, and she swallowed down the lump in her throat as tears once again threatened.

The accusation in his tone speared her conscience and she wondered, not for the first time, if she really could do this alone. She'd thought his harsh words on the beach, after they'd made love in such an explosive and sponta-neous way, had left her with little choice. He'd as good as told her he had no wish to be a father—that the very idea was abhorrent to him.

'Don't try and make it sound like you *want* this baby, Nikos.' She almost hissed the words at him. 'Not when you told me so coldly that you wanted to know of any "consequences."'

'Being a father is not something I had planned.'

He moved away from her, raking his long tanned fingers through his hair, and she sensed his frustration with every nerve in her body.

'Which is why I will return to England and bring up our baby alone.'

She seized on his declaration before he could say anything else, but thoughts of telling her sister almost choked her. How could she tell a woman who wanted a child so desperately that she had made a mistake? That *she* now had that most desired thing? How could she destroy her sister like that?

Anger sparked from his eyes, making her step back away from him, her footsteps faltering in the sand as she stumbled. Before she knew what had happened she was in his arms. The breath seemed to be sucked from her body as the all too familiar scent of Nikos invaded every part of her, setting free yet more memories.

She bit down on her lower lip, anxiety making her brow furrow and her breathing quicken as she looked up at him. His unusual blue eyes sparked with a fiery mix of anger and desire, making her stomach flutter.

'I might not have planned to be a father, but that doesn't mean I'm going to turn my back on my child.'

His words made her heart beat faster, and again the idea of living happily ever after with him flashed before her. Then it was gone, drowned by the reality of their situation. How could they possibly raise a child together? How could they ever be happy after his cold disregard and his lies to conceal his true identity?

She shook her head. 'It will never work, Nikos. Never.'

His hold on her arm tightened, his fingers pressing into

her as he pulled her close. She could feel his breath on her face and fought hard against the overwhelming need to close her eyes and press her lips to his. It was as if she'd stepped back in time, back to the first moment they had met, to the spark of attraction that had leapt to life between them instantly.

She became aware of her phone ringing inside her small handbag and the magic around them evaporated, disappearing to leave stark reality. He let go of her, stepped back, his eyes hard and narrowed, full of suspicion. As the phone ceased its insistent ring an ominous silence settled around them, one so heavy that even the waves seemed to have quietened, stilling in anticipation of what was to come next.

'I am not allowing my child to be brought up in another country. My child will be raised to know its Greek heritage, its Greek family and most importantly its father.'

Each calmly spoken word caressed her face, and even if he'd spoken in Greek she'd have been sure they were words of passion. But she wasn't fooled—they were words of control.

'So where do *I* fit into that?' She pulled back from him, needing the space to think.

'That is what you must decide.' Again it was said in an almost seductive whisper.

'And if I *want* to go back to England?' The question came out as an unexpected hoarse whisper, the pain of it hurting so much.

'Then you must do so—once the child has been born, here in Greece, where it will remain.'

She gasped in disbelief. 'You can't force me to stay. Or expect me to leave without my baby.'

Who *was* this man? Where had the man she'd fallen

in love with gone? This cold, hard and angry man was a total stranger.

'I'm not forcing you to do anything. The choice is yours.'

'No, Nikos.' She stood tall, strength rising up through her. Although she really didn't want her child to grow up with just one parent. She wanted her baby to have all that onlookers thought *she'd* had: two loving and happy parents.

'We will, of course, have to be married.'

He glared at her, hostility emanating from the blue depths of his eyes, and she was thankful they weren't having this conversation in daylight. She didn't want to see the full force of that hostility. At least now it was masked by the quickly descending darkness.

Her phone began to ring again, and her heart hammered loudly as he glanced down at her bag.

'Perhaps you should answer that.'

'No. I can't.'

It was all she could manage as the full implications of what he'd just said hit home. Was she referring to the phone or to marriage? She had no idea, and the words he'd said raced inside her head, confusing her further.

They would have to be married.

Exasperation mixed with fury and fizzed inside Nikos, threatening to explode as he looked down at Serena. Her gorgeous red hair, blown by the warm wind across her face, had created a veil—one she could partially hide behind as she glared back up at him.

'What do you mean, no?'

Nikos thought of the deal he was about to close for the cruise liner company and the effort he'd put into it. Now, trying to reason with Serena, he realised that the deal was a picnic in the sun compared to the negotiation of *this* deal and what was at stake. His child—something he'd never thought he'd have because he'd never allowed himself to want the impossible. He couldn't turn and walk away now. If he did he'd be worse, far worse, than his mother and father.

'I don't know…' she said, shaking her head.

Damn the woman—she was forcing him to strike a deal for his child.

'Well, you'd better think fast.'

He watched her face, saw the ever-changing expressions, holding her captive with his glare.

'Did you ever consider marriage when we had our romantic fling in the summer? Our holiday affair?'

Her voice was sharp and strong, but it was her pale face that told him she was having as much difficulty with this as he was. So she should. What woman would consider giving away her child? One just like his mother.

'You don't even love me.'

'Love has nothing to do with it.' He moderated his tone, aware of his anger rising once more.

'So why do we have to get married?' The disbelief in her voice was more than clear.

'Marriage has never been on my agenda.'

That much was true. After living in the shadow of his parents' marital breakdown he'd written that idea off as a young man, preferring to enjoy the company of woman without complication and commitment. He only sought the pleasure of a woman's company for fun. Purely carnal. Nothing more. Which was exactly what he'd been doing with Serena during her stay on the island.

'And being a father?'

She dropped the question so lightly between them he almost didn't hear it.

'I *will* be a father to my child.' He evaded her question and the truth that lay buried within him. He wanted to be a father—to have his child grow up in a world of love and happiness—but he was sceptical that such happiness actually existed.

'Make no mistake, Serena. My child will not be shuffled between countries like an unwanted Christmas present.'

CHAPTER THREE

SERENA STEPPED AWAY from Nikos—away from the anger of his words. 'I can't talk about this any more.' She needed to put distance between them. 'Maybe we should have this discussion tomorrow?'

He looked at her, unexpected concern in his eyes. 'Perhaps that is best. When you are more rested you will be able to think rationally. Then you will accept that we should marry—for our baby.'

She bristled with indignation at his comment, sure his ability to use English hadn't compromised his choice of words. She *was* perfectly rational, and she had no intention of marrying someone who didn't love her.

'Nothing will change.'

'Where are you staying?'

Nikos asked the question lightly—a little too lightly— arousing her suspicions as to why he appeared to be giving in so easily.

He couldn't be trusted. He'd proved that with his non-revelation about who he really was. She might not have looked him up on the internet before, but she certainly had now. The uneasy feeling that she was dealing with something much bigger than she'd anticipated filled her with dread. He'd concealed his identity, lied to her. *Why?* What would he have to gain by doing that?

'In the same hotel.'

She spoke softly, trying not to think about the nights they'd spent in her room when she'd stayed there before. Why she'd insisted on the same room she didn't know—romantic notions and memories of being there with the man she'd fallen in love with? Or was it because of the night she'd experienced love with Nikos for the first time?

He'd been gentle and kind then, accepting she was innocent but not knowing just how much. She had been sure he was the man she'd waited for. She'd loved him. She'd wanted him to make love to her because then he hadn't been at all like the Nikos who now openly admitted deceiving her and was virtually forcing her into marriage.

'Then we shall go there now and collect your bags.'

He moved towards her, taking her hand in his. She didn't want to follow, to obey his command, but just the touch of his hand against hers sent a sizzle of heat scorching through her and she knew that, whatever the outcome of her visit to the island, there was still unfinished business between them. Her body still craved his, still imagined his caress, his kisses. Stupid as it was, she still loved him.

The hum of music from the bars and restaurants drifted on the warm night air as the sea became an inky blackness, melting into the star-filled sky. Despite the idyllic setting, the idea of walking hand in hand with Nikos felt anything but romantic. Intimidating, maybe—threatening, definitely—but she was powerless to stop it, unable to resist him.

'Nikos!' she gasped, pulling back against him, suddenly regaining her strength, knowing she had to fight. 'What are you *doing*?'

He stopped and looked down at her. His handsome face was partially in shadow, but his eyes sparked like a warrior's, locking with hers, sending a shiver of excitement and apprehension skittering down her spine.

'Taking control.'

The firmness of his voice, still sexy and accented, hinted at the level of discipline he was currently putting on himself.

'Of what? Me?'

She stood tall, facing him in the darkness, hoping that he wouldn't see how unsure she really was, that her voice sounded strong and defiant.

'Of my child.'

She blinked in shock. Did he think that his playing the role of protector would make her fall in line with his plans? That she would marry him and live happily ever after? How could that ever happen when he didn't want her, let alone love her? If she married him her child would grow up knowing it was the mistake that had forced them together—something she *never* wanted a child of hers to feel.

'You don't need to come back to the hotel to do that.'

She really didn't want to be with him at the moment. She needed to think, to re-evaluate things. Nothing had gone as she'd planned. And it was all down to the revelation of his true identity.

His hand in hers felt unnervingly right, but the whole situation was wrong. Confusion at this newly assertive man was mixed with the ever-present heat of desire, fizzing like a newly popped bottle of champagne, and she didn't want to partake of it right now.

'We'll talk again tomorrow.'

'We *will* talk again tomorrow—in Athens.'

He started to walk again, his hand still tightly holding hers, and although she knew she shouldn't want her hand in his she did. A small sliver of hope entered her heart as the sound of the waves was left behind. She walked with him out onto the street and towards the small family-run hotel she adored so much—just as she'd done when she was there before, when things had been different, much more simple.

Then his words registered.

'Athens?' Serena hadn't realised she'd spoken aloud until he turned to look at her, his vivid blue eyes ever watchful.

'My home is there—and my business. We will be leaving in an hour.'

His expression was harsh, his tone firm, and she was so stunned she couldn't say a word. What had made him think she'd leave with him?

'Give me one good reason why I should go anywhere with you when you've lied to me from the very start?'

She couldn't just go—but if he walked away now would she ever be able to forgive herself in years to come when her child wanted to know where its father was?

'There is only one reason, Serena, and it's a *very* good one. You are carrying my child.'

The lights from the hotel shone on his face, highlighting the sharp angles of his cheekbones, making him look so formidable she could imagine him in a boardroom, dominating and controlling everything.

'A child you don't want.'

She flung the accusation at him, feeling hysteria rise inside her. She was too emotionally drained for this—too tired. After almost a day of travelling she just wanted to rest. No, she *had* to rest. But she also had to resist the urge to give in to him, to allow him to take control. He'd lied to her once and she knew from experience that it would happen again. Hadn't her father lied, time and time again?

'There is nothing to discuss. Get your bags. My plane is waiting.'

Inside she seethed with resentment, but she didn't have

the energy to retaliate. He looked down at her and she desperately tried to put up some resistance. It was hard—and not just because she was so tired. Deep down she wanted to be with Nikos, wished she could find a happy-ever-after with him.

She followed him into the hotel, inwardly doing battle with her desire to go with him. Maybe they could recapture what they'd shared such a short time ago? The bright lights of the small reception area made her blink briefly against the glare and she knew that would never happen.

Nikos spoke in hushed Greek to the owner of the hotel and the reality of what was happening rocketed back at her.

She had to go with him—just to sort things out. He was the father of her child and she owed it to the baby to sort things out amicably. But she also owed it to herself not to let him hurt her again, and to do that she had to remain strong.

He turned to face her, his arm outstretched as he drew her close in a show of affection she hadn't been expecting. It was one she was sure was for the hotel owner's benefit.

'We'll be on the plane soon. You can rest there.'

'Rest…?'

Oh, but he was good. She could see the hotel owner smiling at them, as if he was witnessing love's dream couple reunited. Did he *know* Nikos—the real Nikos?

'You must be exhausted.'

His arm about her shoulder pulled her in closer to him and his lips pressed affectionately and familiarly on her forehead, confusing her already muddled emotions further.

'Let's get your things.'

Unable to do anything but play out the charade he'd started, she allowed herself to be led towards the stairs. The lean length of his body was pressed close to her side, sending a spark of awareness all through her. It was so strong she was glad when they reached her room. She be-

latedly rummaged in her handbag for the key, remembering the phone calls she'd not answered. She'd have to deal
with those soon—but first she had an overbearing Greek
to deal with.

'Did you purposely choose the same room?' A hint of
seductive mockery played at the corners of his mouth and
sparkled in his eyes as he looked at her.

As she entered the room she looked about her. It was
much the same as it had been that first night.

'I didn't ask for this room. They must have remembered
me.' She smiled at him, briefly forgetting her intentions,
and for a moment it was like going back to those nights
they'd spent together, teasing and laughing with each other.

She'd been so in love with him, so sure he was *the* man.
She had encouraged his kisses, yearned for his touch and
craved his body, hers seemingly knowing exactly what to
do despite her innocence.

'Is this it? This small case?'

The atmosphere changed as he spoke.

'As I told you, I came to do the decent thing and tell you
to your face. I didn't intend to stay long. It was never as if
we could start again where we'd left off. Not when you'd
made it so clear what your thoughts on being a father were.'

'I did not make any such thing clear.'

He narrowed his eyes and she knew she'd hit a nerve.

'The possibility that those moments on the beach might
have made you a father *horrified* you, Nikos. Don't try to
deny it.' She fired the words at him, feeling herself emotionally stronger again. She wasn't going to allow him to
manipulate her just because he had power and wealth. He
might have hidden that from her when they first met, but
no way would she let him use it against her now.

'That is untrue and you know it.'

He moved closer to her and her heart rate rushed away like a herd of wild horses.

'*Do* I?' She snapped the question out, desperate to hide the effect he was having on her.

His deep, silky voice, heavily accented, did untold things to the heady desire she was trying to suppress. She couldn't let it show. Whatever else he thought, he *had* to think she was completely indifferent to him.

He moved closer to her, his eyes darkening, his accent becoming more pronounced and far too sexy.

'It's still there, isn't it? That sizzle of attraction that kept us here, in this very room, in this very bed, night after night.'

Serena looked at him, her mind racing back to the time they'd spent here, to their first night together. That night he'd kissed her softly, his lips teasing and gentle. She'd known then for certain that this was the man she wanted to give herself to completely. She'd wanted him with such abandon she'd have done anything to show him how much she loved him.

She'd instinctively known that what they'd had was special, that the attraction was one she might never find again. Now, as she stood looking at him, her heart was heavy—because it hadn't been like that for him. It had been nothing more than a passing affair. One he'd hoped he could turn his back on.

She stepped away and looked out of the open window to the sea moving restlessly in the darkness, its salty tang lingering on the warm breeze. This would be her child's heritage—one it might never see if she walked away now. But how could she stay when he didn't want her? Let alone the child she carried?

'Serena…'

His voice was husky and he stood right behind her, the

heat of his body almost too much. She shut her heart against thoughts of what might have been as he placed his hands on her shoulders. Mesmerised by his spell, she turned, looking up into his face. His blue eyes were heavy with desire as they looked into hers, urging her towards him.

She closed her eyes, but that didn't help, and when his lips brushed hers she jumped back and glared at him. 'Don't you *dare* think you can seduce me with kisses this time.'

'I don't need kisses to get what I want.'

He moved closer to her, forcing her against the wall, but she held her ground and maintained eye contact, even though inside she was quaking.

Those hard words had suffocated any lingering illusions of love she'd had. He didn't care about her. He didn't care about the baby. This was all about getting what he wanted.

'So what *is* it you want?' she asked haughtily, testing him. Would he openly admit to being that callous, that cold?

'I want you to come to Athens with me, Serena.'

Each word was full of determination, softened only by the accent that she found so sexy.

She shook her head. 'That's not going to happen, Nikos.'

'Then why are you here?'

She stepped up to him, lifting her chin and glaring angrily at him. 'I came here to tell a fisherman he was to be a father—to tell him that no matter what I'd never stop him from seeing his child. But that fisherman is not you.'

Memories came unbidden to her mind of that night on the beach—the night they'd made love without any thought of contraception. The night they'd created the new life she now held within her. The life whose future she could determine by her choices now.

'It's just as well that I am *not* that fisherman, because

now I can give you what you want—but only if you become my wife. No child of mine will be born illegitimate.'

'You think you have all the power, don't you, Nikos? But you can't *drag* me up the aisle.'

Unnerved by his certainty that he could get what he wanted, she moved away from him and to the door of her room, opening it wide in the hope that he'd leave.

That hope faded instantly.

Nikos remained resolutely still, biting down hard against the anger that coursed through him. How dared she think she could calmly dismiss him from his child's life? He hadn't wanted to be a father, but there was no way he would turn his back on his child—allow it to grow up wondering where he was.

As the challenge of her actions settled around them he knew exactly how he was going to handle this. Serena would be his wife—his *willing* wife—no matter what. His child was going to be born without the stigma of illegitimacy.

He ignored the waves of anxiety rushing through him at the thought of commitment. And he didn't even know if Serena would stay and go along with his plans or if she'd be just like his mother—too selfish to care—and walk away.

'You *will* be my wife. The child you carry is my heir and I will not allow you to keep me from it.'

Hostility poured off her as she stood, rigid and tall, by the open door of the hotel room. With each passing second she was challenging him further, pushing him to limits he'd never thought it possible to go to.

'What are you going to do? *Force* me to marry you?'

The curtness of her tone irritated him further, and he crossed his arms and glared coldly at her.

'I'm going to make you an offer you can't refuse.' Dominance in the boardroom was something he was used to, but overpowering a woman—one he still wanted and desired—was a totally new concept.

'You don't have anything I want, Nikos.'

The hint of confusion in her voice made him raise a brow in speculation. Surely she was curious to hear the terms of his deal?

'If the baby is mine—' he began, but halted as she gasped loudly, her delicate brows furrowed, her soft lips open and her hand against her stomach.

'How *dare* you suggest it isn't?'

'I have no evidence that it is.' He snapped the words at her, feeling her anger as she glared at him, her green eyes sparking.

She spun round so quickly to reach for her handbag that he thought she might fall. She pulled out a small black-and-white photograph.

'Here.' She thrust it at him. 'The evidence you want. That is what you mean, isn't it? Conclusive dates to match the date of that night on the beach?'

'This will do for now, but I would like you to see a doctor here in Greece.'

What kind of fool did she think he was, simply to take her word that she was carrying his child?

He'd seen men cheated into bringing up other men's children, and whilst he would stand by his child he had to *know* that it was his.

Even as the thought entered his mind he knew that it was. She'd been a virgin when she'd met him. He remembered vividly the moment he'd realised the truth. He had cursed aloud, the look of shock on her face forcing him to quell his reaction as he'd focused on giving her as much pleasure as he'd felt. Now all he felt was guilt about questioning her.

'That won't be necessary.' She pushed away from him roughly. 'I have seen doctors in England.'

He looked again at the image, his sharp gaze scanning the information. All the evidence he needed that the baby was his was there, but it was seeing the fuzzy image, knowing it was his baby, that pulled on his heart, creating a tight band across his chest as unfamiliar as if the sea around the island had frozen.

'Even so, you will see a doctor once we arrive in Athens.'

'I'm not going with you, Nikos. And I can't marry you.'

Her voice was filled with emotion, and if he'd been a man with a heart he would have asked why. He would have taken her hand and told her they'd work it out. But he didn't have a heart.

'Once you agree to be my wife, to stay in Greece and to live as a family, I will give you what you want.' He delivered the words in a cool and dominant tone, ignoring the way she visibly flinched.

'I've told you—I don't want anything from you.'

'I'm sure your sister wouldn't like to know you'd turned down a chance of her continuing with her IVF treatment.'

'What?' She crossed the floor and came to stand directly in front of him. 'That is *blackmail*.'

'No, it's getting what I want at whatever price has to be paid.'

'It's blackmail—and totally ruthless.' She hissed the words at him and, despite the situation, he admired her staying power.

'Ruthless, maybe—but it is my only deal.' He laid his final card down and waited for her surrender. 'Take it or leave it.'

'How can you even think I would accept such terms?'

She snatched the scan photo back and looked down at

it, holding it tightly. When she looked up at him the glitter in her eyes bellied the anger he'd provoked.

'Don't go against me, Serena.'

The warning in his voice didn't go unnoticed.

'I'm not going against you. All I want is to do the best for us both—me and my baby.'

Anger shattered around the periphery of his vision and he inhaled deeply, locking his gaze to hers. He'd never expected such challenge, such dismissal of his deal.

'You forget. It is my child too.'

The bristling atmosphere pressed down on Serena as Nikos stood watching—waiting for her answer. She looked again at the scan photo in her hands. The knowledge that she had the power to give the same experience to her sister, or deny her, sickened her. She closed her eyes against the nausea—and against Nikos's merciless scrutiny.

Secretly she'd dreamed of marriage and happy-ever-after, but those dreams had finally died the moment she'd heard Nikos condemn the idea of love. How could she marry a man who not only admitted he hadn't ever wanted to be a father, but one who firmly believed love had nothing to do with marriage?

'But marriage...?' Still stunned by his proposed deal, delivered without a hint of compassion, she could hardly form a sentence. Exasperation and fury raged through her, quelling the nausea of moments ago. 'That's a drastic step, Nikos. What if you meet someone you actually *want* to marry?'

'Marriage has never been on my agenda.'

The icy tone left her in no doubt that he meant it.

'So why marry me?'

Deep down she knew the answer—knew it was because he was opposed to his child being illegitimate. But that went against everything she'd ever wanted for her future. It meant their being forced together because of a baby—a copy of her childhood exactly.

He closed the distance between them, coming so close her heart raced—whether due to the attraction she couldn't completely dismiss or the seriousness of their discussion, she couldn't tell.

'Call me old-fashioned, but my child—my heir—will not be born out of wedlock.' His voice dripped with disdain as he towered over her. 'You must decide, Serena— and right now. My plane is waiting.'

All sorts of scenarios rushed through her mind as he watched her, and she wondered if he could see them playing out. She saw her sister happy and content, with a baby in her arms. Saw her own child looking into its father's eyes and smiling for the first time. These were things she could control just by accepting this bizarre proposal.

An image of herself in Nikos's arms, being kissed with fiery passion, followed swiftly. The passion had existed once, but could it ever turn to love? Could he ever fall in love with her the way she'd fallen in love with him? If they could find that passion again, surely they could find love one day.

'Serena?' he said sternly, pushing her for a decision.

She wanted to rally against him, tell him she needed more time to think—but hadn't she already done plenty of that? And yet if she said yes she'd be doing exactly what he'd suggested when he'd repeated what she'd said— anything to help her sister have a baby of her own.

She saw him draw in a breath of exasperation. Time was running out. If she said yes, went with him now, she would be buying more time to think.

'Very well. We'll do it your way.'

CHAPTER FOUR

As THEY ARRIVED in Athens Serena was still in a state of shock, unable to believe the man she'd fallen in love with could be so cruel.

After the private plane had whisked them from Santorini she'd fully expected a chauffeur-driven car to meet them at the airport, but one of the city's many yellow taxis seemed to be what Nikos wanted.

During the flight she'd played Nikos's words over and over in her mind, each time coming to the same conclusion. She had to accept his so-called deal—for her child and for her sister. She refused to admit that she hoped he might revert to being the man she'd first met and tell her what she most wanted to hear.

She looked across at him as they sat in the taxi. His profile was stern and unyielding. Could this man ever be the Nikos she loved? He looked at her, and even in the semi-darkness as they were driven through Athens at night she felt his icy cold glare.

Instantly she averted her gaze and looked out of the window, amazed by the sights and desperately wishing she wasn't so tired, so confused.

'It's stunning—and so beautiful,' she said as she caught sight of the Acropolis, lit up and standing proud on its rocky vantage point above the city, thankful for its distraction from thinking about the conversation they'd had in her hotel room.

It still hurt, and it proved he didn't have any kind of feelings for her. As far as he was concerned she and his child were nothing more than a commodity to be bargained for.

'It never ceases to please me.' Nikos spoke softly, leaning closer to her as he looked out of the window like a tourist too, seemingly happy to put aside all that had unfolded that evening. 'We should go there one day.'

Serena shrank back in her seat; his words bringing it all back and making her presence on the mainland of Greece sound permanent. It was. She didn't have any other choice.

She pushed those thoughts from her mind, too tired to deal with them any more tonight, but she was still curious as to why Nikos was here when he'd grown up on the island of Santorini. Was that fabrication too?

'How long have you lived in Athens?'

'I came here as a teenager, after I finished school and found myself a job with Xanthippe Shipping. The rest I'm sure you know.' Bitterness edged his words and he too sat back, the beauty of Athens now spoilt for him as much as her. 'My apartment is not far now.'

'I should stay in a hotel,' she volunteered quickly. She'd been too tired to give any thought to where she was going to stay once she was in Athens, but she'd already questioned the sanity of staying with Nikos.

Now she did so again—because of what had been said this evening and the way her body had reacted to him, the way she still wanted and loved him. Staying with him would be a temptation to believe things would work out, when the way he'd reacted earlier told her that was never going to happen.

'No,' he said quickly, then started speaking in Greek to the taxi driver. Within moments they had stopped. He got out and walked around to open her door, his gaze locking with hers.

She stepped out and looked up at the smart modern apartment building blending tastefully with the older buildings around. The street lamps glowed like gold, giving it a magical appearance as well as an affluent one. It was so different from the small whitewashed house nestled on a hillside of Santorini overlooking the sea, which Nikos had pointed out during those blissful two weeks. He'd told her it was hīs home, igniting all sorts of romantic notions in her head, but after tonight's revelations nothing he said could be trusted.

'You are tired and you will stay with me.'

A hint of compassion lingered in the heavily accented words, and if she closed her eyes, pretended the previous hours hadn't existed, she might almost believe he cared.

'I'm not sure that's such a good idea.'

She scrabbled to think of a reason, but couldn't come up with one. They'd already slept together, seen each other naked, so even those excuses didn't fit. The reality was that she did want to be with him. That was why she'd made the journey to Greece instead of calling him. She'd hoped those two weeks together had meant something.

'I'm not going to argue with you any more, Serena. You will stay with me tonight, and after my meeting tomorrow morning we can talk further.'

Inwardly she sighed as the taxi driver pulled away. She was tired—of travelling and of talking. Sleep was what she needed now and the thought of insisting on going to a hotel, then checking in, filled her with dread. She'd stay—tonight, at least—but not in his bed. In the morning she'd be able to think more clearly.

Shouts in Greek caught her attention as a car pulled up alongside them. She turned to look just as Nikos put a protective arm around her, responding in the same language. Just seconds before a camera flash penetrated the night Serena realised they were journalists. Uncomfortable doubt crept over her. Was Nikos such a high-profile figure that they followed him around?

'What do they want?' She glanced quickly at them as they still lingered close by, watching them with suspicion.

She couldn't keep the sceptical edge from her voice as he held the main door to the apartment building open for her and she walked into a bright lobby, the white walls a stark contrast to the darkness outside.

'They wanted to know who you are.' He took his keys from his pocket then pressed the button to call the lift.

'Why am *I* of any importance?' She frowned as she watched the numbers above the lift counting down the floors, trying to appear unfazed by the event.

He sighed and she felt his gaze on her face.

'It has been an obsession with them for the past year or so. The more successful my business becomes, and the more unattached I remain, the more determined they are to dig something up.'

'So what did you tell them?'

Her heart began to thump harder as he looked into her eyes. The depths of his were darkening to a sultry blue, which made her stomach flutter wildly. She cursed her body—and her emotions—for falling under the spell of his charm.

'The truth.'

The lift doors swished open. He walked inside and then stood looking at her, the spark of mischief in his eyes and the quirk of a smile on his lips almost her undoing.

Determined not to let him see just how easily he could crash through her defences, she marched in after him.

'What *is* the truth?'

'That we are engaged.'

Serena wasn't sure if it was the movement of the lift or the words he'd just spoken that made her stomach lurch and her head spin. She clutched at the handrail inside the lift and closed her eyes against a wave of nausea.

Nikos moved quickly as Serena's face paled. Her knuckles whitened as she gripped the handrail and he wrapped an arm around her, pulling her close against him. He could feel her sliding down, so scooped her up into his arms just as the lift doors opened.

Furious that she'd allowed herself to become so exhausted by travelling all the way to Greece alone, risking his child, he marched towards his door. With each step he took he could feel her body against his, and an unknown emotion of protectiveness swept over him, but he pushed aside the unfamiliar sensation, not wanting to know why or how.

Swiftly, and with ease, he unlocked the front door and angled himself so he could negotiate the doorway without letting her go. Full of concern, he looked down at her just as her eyelashes fluttered open. Relief filled him as green eyes, full of questions and shock, met his.

'You are supposed to do this *after* we are married...' Her voice was weak, more like a throaty whisper, and her pale face looked anxious.

'I always do things *my* way, Serena.'

The words came out harder than he'd intended, and he felt her sharp intake of breath as he held her.

She wriggled in his arms as he made his way into the open-plan apartment. The view of the city lights twinkling beneath the floodlit Acropolis didn't move him this evening. Concern for Serena and his baby took precedence, as did his guilt at flying her back here tonight.

He could have made the flight alone, attended his meeting, then gone back for her—but instinct had warned him against that. Everything she'd said had made him sure she wouldn't meekly be waiting for him to return. He knew she was only here because of the deal he'd offered and nothing more.

Satisfied that the child she carried was his, he was not going to let her go easily. He was prepared to do anything to create a family for his child. The kind of family he'd craved as a boy and thought he'd never have. It didn't matter what excuses or what reasons she gave him, he was going to give his child what he'd never had.

'You can put me down now.'

She pushed her hands against his chest and he heard the strength in her voice returning. As did the spark in her eyes, making them resemble the bright green leaves of spring.

'It was the lift that made me dizzy. It's been a long day.'

'I will order in something to eat, then you can rest.'

He let her slide from him, feeling every delectable curve of her against his body, arousing all the passion he'd been suppressing since he'd got the message from her this morning. He couldn't allow lust to complicate things—certainly not his inability to control it. Lust-filled desire had already caused enough problems.

She nodded and walked towards the balcony doors. Glad of her acceptance of the situation, he slid open the large glass doors, letting the buzz from the city streets flow in.

'Enjoy the view.'

She turned, her gaze meeting his, and another pang of guilt rushed over him. She looked so tired—but there was still a hint of the feisty woman who'd met him just a few hours ago. Their differences were far from settled. But this wasn't something which could be settled overnight. This was much more, and the full implications of what Serena's presence in Greece meant finally hit him.

What he did now would affect not only his life but his child's—and Serena's. Despite that, he didn't regret the deal he'd put to her. It had presented itself so innocuously that at first he hadn't seen it as important, but he knew that without it Serena would have walked away from him for ever, taking his child too.

It was far too close to the pain of his own childhood, and thoughts of his father's blatant denial of his existence rushed forward like the tide with gale force winds behind it. He'd watched him withdraw until he could no longer look at his only son. There was no way he was going to deny *his* child existed, ignoring it like an inconvenience.

For the first time ever he knew he wanted to be different. Better. He wanted to be a father in every way—to be there each day and each night for his son. But to do that he needed Serena to stay with him…something his mother had been unable to do.

Those thoughts jarred inside him as he made a call to organise an evening meal to be brought in, trying not to think beyond that moment. He joined her on the balcony, where the warm evening air was finally cooling as he stood next to her.

It had been the same kind of warm weather the night he and Serena had walked along the beach for the last time. That night should have been for them to say goodbye, but one kiss had turned it into so much more.

His pulse began to pound like a drum and the hum of desire warmed his blood as he remembered the night that had changed his life for good.

He'd taken Serena in his arms, knowing it was time to say goodbye, to push her away, to deny himself the love which shone in her eyes each time they met. She deserved more than a cold-hearted man such as him: a man who could not and would not allow love into his life—and never into his heart.

She'd whispered his name as she'd kissed him, and he'd held her so tight, deepening the kiss, his hands caressing her body, committing to memory each and every curve. As passion had swept them away the champagne supper he'd organised as a farewell meal had lain abandoned beside them on the blanket. With the moon and the stars shining above them he'd made her his one last time, without thought of anything else.

'Nikos, I love you,' she'd whispered as his pulse rate had returned to normal.

Every drop of blood within him had frozen, crystallising in his veins, choking him. It wasn't possible. He was unlovable. Hadn't his mother said as much? Then, as the ice had splintered around them, he'd realised what had happened. He hadn't used any form of contraception. He had broken the one rule he'd always followed and in doing so had exposed himself to the possibility of fathering a child.

Before he'd known how he'd been standing on the sand, looking down at her, with the blanket rumpled beneath her and the glasses of champagne spilt. Fury had boiled inside him at how easily he had been distracted. What if this moment of mad lust resulted in a child? He didn't want to be a father. He *couldn't* be a father.

As memories of that night rushed through him he knew that whatever he'd previously thought he could not turn his back on his child—ever. But that night he'd spoken starkly, each word more forceful than the last. 'If there are consequences of what has just happened you *will* tell me.'

Anger had blinded him to anything else, and the evening he'd planned had dissolved around them. She'd got up, dusted the sand from her clothes and looked at him, her beautiful face paling. Before he'd been able to say anything else she'd fled, running from him as if he was the devil.

The damning words of love she'd said had replayed in his mind like a haunting melody, and with a cowardice he'd never before known he had remained where he was, watching her run from him.

Now she stood resolute and courageous on his balcony, with her gaze meeting his and the gold glow from the city casting shadows around her. For the first time he'd recalled what she'd said that night. *That she loved him.* Fear gripped him—not because of what she'd said, but because briefly he'd believed he could love her. If only his childhood experience of that powerful emotion had been different.

'Excuse me. I will get the food,' he said quickly, grateful of the distraction.

He didn't want to think about what those words had meant, much less acknowledge them.

Exhaustion swept over Serena and she knew she couldn't eat another bite of the delicious meal or engage in any more small talk. She had to sleep. She couldn't put it off any longer and wished she'd insisted on a hotel. At least that would have given her some much needed time alone.

'I'll show you to your room,' Nikos said, and he stood up, uncannily reading her thoughts.

He dominated the room, looking so handsome her heart hammered, but she couldn't let that sway her. She had to remember what he was capable of.

She should feel relieved that she was to have her own room—that he wasn't assuming they were going to continue where they'd left off. But she didn't. It was like a rejection of her as a woman.

'Thank you,' she said, reassured by the patience in his tone. It still hurt, but she kept up a facade of defiance, not wanting him to know how disappointed she was and how much she wished things could be different.

Isolation crammed in on her. If only she'd been able to talk to her sister—confide in someone sensible and rational. Sally, eight years older, had always been her place to go for advice, which made the secret she now kept even harder to endure. Especially as it was the very thing Sally desired most in the world. Marrying Nikos was the only way to give that hope back to Sally.

'I will be leaving early in the morning. I have an important meeting tomorrow. Relax, enjoy the apartment and I will be back at lunchtime.'

His blue eyes were full of concern, and for a moment she thought she saw genuine warmth in them. He stood holding the door open as she walked past him and she caught a hint of his aftershave. Citrus aromas mingled with crisp pine, reminding her of what it was like to be close to him.

'Sleep well.'

He was leaving her alone—tonight and tomorrow. All sorts of scenarios, from boarding the first UK-bound plane to luxuriating here in his apartment, filled her mind. 'Aren't you worried I will leave?'

'You may do whatever you wish, Serena, but I'm sure you want your sister's happiness as much as I want to be a part of my child's life.'

'You're hateful,' she whispered harshly, the reminder of his terms knocking out any misplaced hope she might have been nurturing.

'Just remember this: no matter where you go, I will find you.'

A hard edge of warning crept into his voice and she swallowed back her retort. Her heart thumped at the implication of his words.

'Goodnight, Nikos.' She stood behind the door of her

room, using it as a shield against the darkness of his glittering eyes.

'Goodnight, Serena.' He turned and walked away, his footsteps on the marble floor as insistent as his voice.

She closed the door and took her phone from her handbag. Two missed calls from Sally. Her heart plummeted with dread. Could she say anything to her without blurting out the sorry tale of her and Nikos? She pressed the button to dial and waited as the call was connected, relieved when Sally answered almost immediately.

'Serena, where are you? Not in Greece, by any chance, with your handsome fisherman?'

The teasing tones of Sally's words made her smile, despite the weight of what she wanted to confide in her sister.

'As a matter of fact, yes.'

'That's *such* good news. I've been worried about you.'

Guilt washed over Serena. The last thing Sally needed was more worry than she already had, but she'd always been mothered by her elder sister. She had stepped in when their parents had been too busy avoiding each other instead of being around for their daughters.

'I'm fine—but what about you?'

'It's not good news, I'm afraid.'

The wobble in her sister's voice nearly broke Serena's heart. She sat down on the bed, her dizziness making the room slowly turn.

'I'm sorry, Sally.' She closed her eyes, feeling the cage Nikos had used to trap her shrinking. There wasn't any escape now. She had to accept his barbaric terms.

'It was the last time. I'm never going to be a mother now.'

She could hear Sally's pain searing at her from across the miles and wished she was there to hug away her hurt. Instead she placed her hand over her still flat stomach and a tear slid down her cheek. Guilt mixed with grief was threatening to overpower her. She couldn't confide in her now. Not tonight, anyway.

'We'll find another way. I promise.'

Serena's body had turned cold. There was only one other way.

'Now, you get back to your Greek,' her sister said, and she could hear her effort to remain bright. 'And, Serena…?'

Serena's breath caught in her throat as she registered the pause in the conversation. 'Yes?'

'Stop using Mum and Dad's marriage as an example. Create something better for yourself. If you find love, grab it and hang on to it. Be brave, Serena. Be *brave*.'

Serena nodded, not able to form any kind of reply, knowing her sister's advice was well meant. But what if the man you loved didn't want to love *you*?

More tears prickled in her eyes and she knew she had to end the call. 'I will. See you soon.'

With Sally's goodbye ringing in her head, she cut the connection and lay on the bed, desperately needing to sleep. But her sister's advice played over and over again in her head. Were her parents and their unhappy marriage the reason why she'd never had a long-term relationship? Had that been why she'd pushed everyone away?

With shock, she realised the truth of her sister's words and knew it was time to stop hiding from life—and love. The father of her child might not love her, but she loved him. Was that enough—for her and her child?

Other people's happiness now rested on it. It would have to be.

CHAPTER FIVE

NIKOS'S MOOD WAS dark as he called a halt to his meeting. It had been intense, and there had been moments when his usual ruthless and determined manner had been nudged sideways by thoughts of the redhead he'd left sleeping peacefully in his apartment.

Yesterday his life had been normal. Uninvolved and normal. Now, with Serena's return, it had been turned completely inside out.

Impatience to end the meeting and return home had made him even more aggressive in his approach to the final stages of the takeover than he would usually be. Abruptly he'd put his deal on the table, insisting further negotiations were off the agenda. He wanted the company badly, but right now he had far more pressing things to worry about.

The most important deal he had to strike was keeping his child in his life—and to do that he had to ensure Serena became his wife. The cruise company could wait.

As he arrived at his apartment several photographers rushed forward and he cursed what he'd told that one opportune photographer last night, when he'd been asked who Serena was. Not for the first time when he was around her, he hadn't thought of the consequences of his actions. He had known his playboy reputation and current business dealings would make him tabloid fodder.

'Where is your fiancée?'

They hassled him, their Greek words fast and furious, their cameras clicking.

'Did you get the deal as well as the girl?' Another asked as he reached the front doors of his apartment block, with the traffic rushing by almost drowning out the bombardment of questions.

'I do not have answers to your questions yet, gentlemen, but soon.'

He used the charm he was renowned for, keeping a cool exterior. Inside, emotions he was unfamiliar with mixed with irritation.

He pushed open the door, making sure it was firmly shut behind him as he walked into the cool quietness of the lobby. Several flashes bounced off the white walls as he waited for the lift, his back to the doors and reporters, so as not to give them the photo they wanted.

Since Serena's text had come through nothing had gone to plan. The business deal he had previously been sure of clinching now hung in the balance, due to his earlier hardened dealings, and he had no idea if Serena would still be there. He'd left her alone purposely, to think through the offer he'd put to her and also give her ample opportunity to leave and get a flight home. Had that been what the reporters meant when they'd asked where she was? Had they witnessed her leave? Seen her get a taxi to the airport?

The thought of being denied his child sent a storm-surge of anger charging through him. Even if she chose to run she was never going to be able to keep him from his child.

The lift swiftly moved upwards. A small part of him wished it would stop, and along with it the whole world, so that he didn't have to witness and acknowledge that the only woman who'd made him want more had walked away from him. Just as his mother had.

Outside the door of his apartment he paused. Why did this feel so raw? Why was it like standing on the beach as a six-year-old boy waiting, hoping, for his mother to return? For a long time he hadn't believed his mother had meant it when she'd told him she didn't love him and that he'd be better off without her, but her continued absence had backed up her cold claim.

Enough. The word snapped in his head like an arrow from a bow. Now was not the time to dwell on the past. He couldn't influence that any more, but he could control the present.

With renewed determination he unlocked the door and walked in.

The balcony doors were open and sounds from the street drifted up and into the apartment. He strode towards the balcony, feeling as if his heart was in his throat. He wasn't quick enough to smother a sigh of relief at the sight of Serena, sitting in the shade, typing away on her laptop.

So she was preparing her story, was she? What headline would she use?

'Working?' He threw the word at her gruffly, accusation bound tightly up within it.

She physically jumped, her head turning towards him so fast her silky red hair splayed out like a fan around her before falling neatly to her shoulders in a way that snared his attention, reminding him of the times he'd seen it spread across a pillow.

She smiled at him, her green eyes sparkling and alert after a night's sleep. 'I wasn't expecting you back for hours yet—a busy man like you. What with your shipping company to run and the glamorous social life you lead.'

The sarcasm in her voice was not lost on him and he moved closer, lured by something he didn't yet understand—something he didn't want to understand.

She returned her attention to her laptop, saving her work before closing it down, and then stood up. His eyes were drawn to her figure and the way her pale green dress hugged her breasts and skimmed her waist. He would never have known she carried his child if she hadn't told him.

'It sounds like you've been doing some research.' He should feel irritated that she'd been here in his home, researching him on the internet, but instead he was shocked to find the thought amused him. 'You could just *ask* me about my life. After all, you can't believe everything the papers say.'

'You weren't honest with me when we first met, so why should I believe anything else you tell me?'

The light tone of her voice was in complete contrast to the stern look on her face and he fought the urge to pull her to him, feel her body against his and kiss her. He shouldn't desire her, but he did.

'You probably know all there is to know now.'

He glanced out at the Acropolis, busy with people visiting in the sunshine. The thought that they should go there wandered idly through his mind.

'Hmm,' she said, and walked towards him, testing his restraint too much. 'It's a shame I prefer the fisherman I first met to the businessman I now see. But he wasn't real—was he, Nikos?'

He moved closer, clenching his hands against the urge to take her in his arms and kiss her. Inside, the need to show her he was the same man grew stronger by the second. His guard slipped like a sail unfurled just before the wind filled it. He wanted to tell her he was the same man inside, that he desired her as much as he had when they'd first met, but that would be showing his hand—something he couldn't ever do.

Then, as if the sail had been filled with the ocean wind, his guard was back, rising higher than ever.

'Right now I'm not just a businessman. I'm also a fiancé who needs to take his intended bride shopping for a ring.' He growled the words as his control was tested far more than he'd ever thought possible. What *was* it about her that made him like this?

'Out of necessity!' She tossed the words lightly at him as she walked back into the apartment.

Of course she was right. She was carrying his child, his heir, and he had every intention of doing the right thing. No matter the cost, emotionally or financially, his child would be born within marriage.

Marriage.

The word bounced around inside his head like a shout echoing in a cave, taunting him. Marriage was something he'd never aspired to. There had been no need. He'd never wanted to be a father. But one spontaneous and out of control night had changed all that.

'We cannot be married without first being engaged.' His voice was rough and hard as he pushed back emotions from the past that he couldn't deal with now. He'd always looked forward—looking back only caused pain.

'Perhaps you'd better look at the headlines today.' She smiled sweetly and made her way to the kitchen.

He watched her as she poured iced water into two glasses and handed him one.

'The reporters last night have taken you at your word, judging by their photos.'

His comment last night might have been made without the thought he usually gave dealing with the press, but it had certainly sparked a furore of media interest. He just wished he'd seen it first.

'Is that a problem?'

'Of course it is. You've made certain I have no option but to accept your absurd deal. But I hate you for it Nikos—with all my heart.'

Serena saw the colour drain from Nikos's face. Last night she hadn't realised there had been calculated planning behind making such an admission to the press, but now she did. It had been made to remove that tiny window of escape, to force her to accept his deal.

She hadn't arrived looking for marriage—just the opportunity to do the right thing and tell him face-to-face. After her talk with Sally last night she knew deep down she wanted to be with Nikos, to raise his child. But he must never know that—not when he could use her so cruelly after all they'd shared.

It was perfectly clear he didn't want commitment, and if their last night together hadn't resulted in pregnancy she would never have seen him again. Somewhere deep inside she'd known that all along, but now he was forcing her into a marriage neither wanted. A marriage just the same as her parents had had, until their divorce a few years ago. One for the sake of their child—and *she'd* been the one who'd paid the price.

She inhaled deeply. Her child might not have been planned, but she'd never let her child think he or she was a mistake, never make it feel guilty for forcing its parents to be together. The idea of marriage to Nikos had been a far-fetched dream, but now it was a harsh reality that would enable her sister's dreams to come true. A high price, but one she would willingly pay if it meant Sally becoming a mother.

'I have a charity party to attend this evening. I need to talk with some business acquaintances. You will come too.'

He'd recovered his composure quickly. The ruthless

businessman was well and truly back in control and today he looked even more so than he'd ever done. The fisherman she'd met wasn't evident at all. The tailored suit that hugged his body with agonising perfection and the crisp white of his shirt shouted professionalism, but the expensive watch on his wrist and gold signet ring screamed success.

Before seeing him this morning she'd already decided she had no choice but to stay, to give marriage to him a chance not just for her child but for Sally. It was Sally's advice that had taken the sting out of Nikos's deal, warning her she mustn't base her life on her parents' marriage. She had to find her own happiness and she owed it to her child at least to try.

Despite that, she couldn't keep a cutting remark from leaving her lips. 'In what capacity? Your fiancée—as you told those reporters last night?

His blue eyes darkened. Glittering sparks shot from them and he set his lips in that all too familiar line that she was fast becoming accustomed to. It was something she'd never seen the fisherman she'd fallen in love with do.

'Of course. We are to be married—that is why you are still here, is it not?'

'I'm still here because it helps my sister.' She threw her retort back at him, infuriated by his arrogance.

'I will buy you a ring so big there will not be any questions as to my intentions towards you.'

His acerbic tone cut deep, but she didn't let it show. Instead she took a sip of water. The ice clinking in the glass as her hands shook almost gave away how much his words had hurt.

'After those newspaper headlines that will save a lot of awkward questions.'

Buying an engagement ring with a man in such a harsh

mood wasn't at all what she'd hoped for. Even though theirs wasn't going to be a marriage made out of love, she'd hoped the desire and passion they'd once shared would count for something.

'I had no idea the story would get out. It won't help my current negotiations if I'm seen to be going back on my word to the woman I've proposed to. Are you ready to go right now?'

'I'm ready,' she said—though she wondered if she was ever going to be ready to enter into a loveless marriage. It was her parents all over again. Their unhappiness had been her fault, and now she was going to lay that guilt on her own child—but with Sally's happiness at stake she had little choice…for now at least.

Half an hour later, having been driven through the rush of Athens traffic, she was in an exclusive and very expensive jewellers with an attentive Nikos at her side. His acting skills were incredible, and he lovingly laid his arm around her shoulders as she tried the biggest diamond ring she'd ever seen on her finger.

The assistant gushed, but her Greek words were totally lost on Serena. It was an amazing ring—a big show of wealth—but it wasn't at all what she wanted.

'No,' she said decisively, and the assistant's smile slipped. 'This is too big…too expensive.'

'Expense doesn't come into it.'

His sexy voice was deep, almost a whisper, sending shivers of awareness down her spine. She reminded herself that it was all for show. She mustn't for one moment think he cared. He didn't.

'Very well—it's too big.' She looked at him, unable to keep the confrontation from her eyes. 'This is much more to my taste.'

She picked up a small but beautiful emerald ring, and

was about to try it on when Nikos took it from her, held her hand and slid it on to her finger.

She looked at him and her breath caught in her throat. The intensity in his eyes warmed her from the inside out. Her heartbeat raced and her stomach fluttered. His gaze, darkening to resemble the sea at night, held hers, and she might have been back on the beach, just before they'd made love. His eyes had swirled with the same ardent passion then too.

'This is the ring.'

His voice was husky, his accent heavy, making her heart pound harder.

'Serena, will you marry me?'

She swallowed hard, aware that her breathing had deepened and each breath was harder to come by. Would he think she was acting the part too? She certainly hoped so, because he must never find out how much she loved him.

'Yes.'

She responded with the answer she knew he wanted for the sake of acting the part. Would she have given the same answer if he'd asked her last night, instead of blackmailing her with something as cruel as her sister's happiness?

His lips brushed hers so briefly she wondered if it had happened. Her sigh of pleasure couldn't break the connection that arced between her and Nikos at that moment. Serena couldn't breathe as he continued to hold her hand, his fingers warm against hers. It felt so real, so passionate, so loving.

It's just pretence, she reminded herself sternly.

Nikos's heart beat faster than he'd ever known. What was the matter with him? He was getting carried away with the moment. He looked into her eyes again and lifted her fingers to his lips. The green of her eyes was flashing

brighter than the emerald on her finger and he wanted her
with a force that stunned him.

'The gemstone of the goddess Venus. A symbol of
hope,' the assistant said in stilted English, her words breaking the spell.

Serena pulled away from him, her eyes downcast and
her long lashes sweeping down, locking him out.

'Then it is a perfect choice,' he said softly, and lifted her
chin, forcing her to look into his eyes once more.

'It brings lovers closer if the giver's motive is pure love.'
The assistant continued with her sales talk.

What did it mean if his motive was convenience coupled
with lust? He looked into Serena's face. Her porcelain-like
skin was faintly flushed, but her gaze held his boldly. Was
she wondering the same?

Before he had time to think, to rationalise his actions, he
lowered his head and brushed his lips over hers. A startled
gasp of shock broke against his lips, lighting the fire that
only she had ever truly ignited. He wanted to pull her close,
to kiss her harder. He wanted so much more but propriety
surfaced. Now was not the time or the place.

'Nikos…' she whispered quickly, and pressed her palms
against his chest, pushing him away, her thoughts obviously echoing his.

He smiled down at her, took her hand in his and then
turned to the assistant to pay for the ring. All the time he
held her hand, keeping her at his side. He could feel the
warmth of her body invading his and wished they were
anywhere else but here. The passion that had exploded between them when they had first met was still burning—and
it was becoming stronger and harder to resist.

The deal they'd struck had just become very interesting.

'We have more shopping to do yet,' he said as they
emerged into the sunshine of the afternoon.

She pulled him to a stop, but he didn't let go of her hand. Instead he pulled her closer as the desire he'd suppressed in the shop simmered through him.

'We don't need to buy anything else. A ring is enough for anyone to believe we're getting married. Nobody has to believe it's because we're in love.'

His brows rose in question and the word *love* all but doused the fire that burned for her. He didn't worry about people questioning if they were in love—it was his business reputation, his ability to keep his word, that mattered most.

'We agreed that marriage was best in the circumstances.'

'Agreed?' She glared up at him, her eyes flashing with challenge.

'You came to Athens with me. You obviously agreed with my terms. And as I told the press last night we were engaged you now need to be seen wearing my ring. Do you think my business associates will take me seriously otherwise? Having people believe we are "in love" has nothing to do with it. I want people to see that I honour my word, my promise and most importantly my obligations to the child you carry.'

Irritation surged forward, overriding all his previous emotions. It was for the best, he thought as he looked down into her face, at her eyes shrouded in confusion. If he had to keep playing the role of lover it would lead to temptation and desire, which would only complicate the situation.

'Do you *really* think we agreed on marriage? It was more of a case of you deciding it would happen and instigating it with little regard for anyone else.'

Her words were sharp and she stood her ground, and he became aware that they were attracting the attention of passers-by.

'Come,' he said, in a growly voice that did little to hide his jumbled emotions. 'You must get something to wear at the party tonight.'

'I don't need anything new.'

Her voice rose a little and her shoulders straightened, warning him of her intention to go against him.

'As my bride-to-be you will be expected to look amazing. Anything less just isn't acceptable.'

He looked at her, seeing her confusion become quickly masked by spirit.

'I can't compete with the models you've dated. Even the most fabulous dress won't do that.'

'I do not expect you to compete with anyone,' he said calmly, and moved closer to her, dominating her with his height. But again she held her ground and looked up at him, her lips set in a pout of annoyance, just begging to be kissed.

It was an offer he couldn't refuse. Before she had time to move he pulled her close with his free arm, pressing her against him while still holding her hand. His lips burned as they met hers. Their initial resistance melted almost immediately and he felt her body relax and mould against his.

He broke the kiss and pulled back from her. He had to stop kissing her in public. He promised himself that next time it would be in the privacy of his apartment, where he could give in to the carnal hunger she provoked.

He glanced up and down the crowded street and found what he was looking for—an exclusive boutique. 'This way. Unless you want me to kiss you again.'

To his relief the threat worked, and she fell into step beside him as they made their way up the busy street. As soon as they entered the shop assistants came forward, as keen to help as the one in the jeweller's. He informed them in Greek of what Serena needed and turned to her, amused by the stunned look on her face.

'I have calls to make, but they know what I want.'

'What *you* want?' Incredulity rang out from each word and those lovely green eyes widened with shock.

'Yes, what *I* want. I will see you in an hour.'

He turned and left the shop…before he kissed the look of astonishment from her beautiful face.

Serena fumed as he turned and walked away. Just who did he think he was? And how had she ever fallen for his gentle fisherman act? Had she been so blinded by her love for him she hadn't seen even a *hint* of his lies? She'd lived her life watching her father lie, hiding his love affairs behind his work. Was she now going to be forced to live with a man who lied to achieve his goals?

Further thoughts were brushed aside as the assistants all but whisked her away. Dress after dress was held up to her, and the rapid exchange of Greek almost made her head spin, but when they finally agreed on a dress she couldn't help but smile with pleasure.

She tried it on and looked at her reflection. The pale green silk skimmed over her curves and the small swell of her stomach would never be noticed—not even by the most observant. Her eyes looked vibrant and alive, and her hair contrasted beautifully with the dress, lying on bare shoulders. It was perfect. Maybe she *could* be as glamorous as the women she'd seen Nikos spread all over the internet with that morning.

Apprehension rushed in, knocking the confidence from her. Would Nikos notice her—desire her as he'd once done—like this? The thought ambled around her mind only to be forced out. The ruthless businessman that Nikos truly was wouldn't notice her, but she hoped the man she'd met—the loving fisherman—would.

Reluctantly she removed the dress and put her sundress on again. The glamorous and bright-looking woman she'd seen reflected in the mirror disappeared. In her place stood a normal and very plain woman—one who would never have turned the head of a Greek billionaire. He'd been amusing himself at her expense, letting her fall in love with him whilst she was researching her article, safe in the knowledge that she would go home and never return.

But she *had* returned.

She'd returned carrying his child and he'd been forced to admit who he really was. He'd dragged her into his world of luxury and wealth and tonight she would play him at his own game. She would be someone she wasn't. She would make him want her. And then, like in a fairy tale, she would revert to her usual self by dawn.

CHAPTER SIX

NIKOS WAS STUNNED into silence as Serena came out of the guest room, ready for the party. He knew he was staring at her like an unpractised youth. But what man wouldn't? He'd never seen her dressed like this, and wondered how she'd ever thought she couldn't compete with other women. She'd outshine them completely—and not just in *his* eyes.

She was utterly gorgeous and he wished he hadn't accepted the party invitation. Right now all he wanted was to be alone with her, to taste the desire they'd shared and experience the passion once more.

The uncertainty in the green depths of her eyes tugged at his heart. A heart he had thought to be frozen since the moment his mother had walked out of his life, showing him the cruel side of love. But his heart would have to remain icy-cold, devoid of emotion. It would be better that way—for both of them.

His attention was caught by her heels daintily tapping out a beat as she walked towards him—a beat that matched the throb of desire within him, which was increasing with each second.

'I had no idea what was needed for this evening, but the shop assistants assured me, as best they could in Greek, that this was it. I trust it meets with your approval?'

He let his gaze blatantly slide down her, marvelling at her resolute composure. 'It is more than everything I anticipated,' he said forcefully. The words *You look so beautiful* were suppressed, along with the weak-willed wish that things were different.

'I don't want to stand out too much,' she said, and she lowered her gaze to fiddle with her clutch bag.

A surge of unfamiliar protectiveness flared within him. 'You will stand out—but it will be for the right reasons.'

'It will be bad enough not understanding what's being said all night, without wearing the wrong thing.'

'Bad enough?'

Most women he knew would be desperate for the chance to be bought a pretty dress and taken out for the evening—but Serena wasn't most women. He was fast realising she was different. Too different.

'The headlines,' she said quickly, then looked at him, a hint of disappointment in her eyes. 'Have you forgotten that all of Greece now believes we are engaged?'

'No, I have not—and I will be with you at your side all night.'

His swift reply banished any further discussion.

He *did* have business connections to make, and originally his intention had been simply to halt any rumours that might be growing about her arrival. But as he looked down at Serena he knew having her at his side would make a nice change from the frivolous models he usually chose as company for such occasions. Not one of the women he'd dated had ever affected him the way Serena had—and still did.

If he was honest with himself it went back to their time in Santorini—to a time when his guard had been lowered... a time when he'd tasted what might have been if only his life had been different.

'We will leave now, if you are ready?'

She nodded, briefly looking nervous before smiling. 'I'm ready.'

The party had been underway for some time when they arrived, and he felt Serena tense as they entered the large room. The hum of chatter continued, but he was aware of speculative glances being cast their way, and whispers that were far from discreet.

With his arm around her, and his hand resting at her waist, he guided her through the throng of the elite of Athens society. It seemed the fundraiser had pulled people in from far and wide.

'Nikos!'

He paused at the mention of his name and saw Christos Korosidis, the head of a rival shipping company. In the boardroom they would be enemies, but in the buzz of a party—especially a fundraising event—they would assume the air of friendship.

'So the rumour is true?' Christos said, his admiring gaze sweeping over Serena, sending a zip of totally alien jealousy hurtling through Nikos. 'I would never have thought you were the marrying kind, Nikos.'

He could hear the conjecture in the other man's voice and knew Serena's sudden appearance in his life was causing as much controversy as his bid to take over Adonia Cruise Liners. A company Christos also had his sights on.

Nikos wondered if Christos would use the current news of his engagement to slip in under the radar and make another bid. He should have been angry at the idea, but he wasn't. If the deal failed—it failed.

This was a completely new way for him to look at things. He didn't *care* if Christos put a new offer in and won. Right now all that mattered was his child, his heir, and in order to be a part of its life he had to keep Serena at his side. As far as he was concerned his marriage was the most important deal right now. It would legitimise his son and heir. Not that he'd ever hint at that to Christos.

'Appearances can be deceptive,' he said with a smile as he took a glass of champagne and handed it to Serena.

She frowned, making it clear she wasn't drinking alcohol, but took it from him, holding it with elegantly manicured hands. In that second he cursed his stupidity. She might not have chosen to disclose the reason for her return to Christos, but he was an astute man. Her reaction to the champagne hadn't gone unnoticed.

'Nikos and I met several months ago in Santorini.'

Serena's soft voice broke through his turmoil and his body heated as she moved closer against him, her smile distracting Christos instantly.

'Serena has thankfully just returned to Greece,' Nikos said, and looked down at her when she glanced up at him. He brushed his lips over her forehead lightly, then turned his attention back to his sparring partner in business, trying to ignore the warmth that flooded through him. 'And not a moment too soon.'

Beside him he felt Serena stiffen and try to pull away, but he kept her close. Her light floral scent was invading his senses, stirring them evocatively and unbalancing him further. But it was as she remained stiffly at his side that the implications of his words sank in. All he'd meant was that he hadn't been able to stop thinking about her—which in itself had been truthful—but what he'd just said could be taken another way. Or was that his guilty conscience at work…?

'Nice to have met you.' Christos bestowed another charming smile on Serena and moved on in his mission to circulate.

Nikos inhaled slowly. He had to regain control of his emotions. He was more distracted than he'd ever been by Serena, and wondered how long he'd be able to keep up the pretence of being a caring fiancé when all he wanted was to claim her as his in every sense.

'That went well.'

Serena's feisty remark cut off all thought and he turned his attention back to her, taking the glass of untouched champagne from her and placing it on a nearby table.

'Was that your way of covering up the truth?'

'If I wanted to cover up the truth, as you put it, I would adopt a very different tactic—one that would leave nobody in any doubt about the irresistible passion that has brought you back to Greece.'

'And that would be what?'

'I'd kiss you deeply and passionately, right here, for all to see.'

His blood heated as she glared up at him, her lips parted, almost daring him to carry out his threat. It was all he could do *not* to pull her into his arms and kiss her—deeply and passionately.

Her brows rose and a teasing smile lit up her eyes. 'You wouldn't dare…'

'You're playing a dangerous game, Serena.' The thud of desire quickened, and without thinking of where they were he stepped closer to her. 'Is that what you want me to do? Kiss you?'

'No, I don't.'

Her firm words pulled him back, then he laughed softly.

Did she think playing such games in public would force him to show there was more to their marriage than an accidental pregnancy?

'I know you don't really want me. You just want your child—but without any scandal. I can see that now. And for the record,' she said flippantly, her eyes flashing with provocation, 'you wouldn't *dare* kiss me here. At least not in the way you're threatening.'

'Don't challenge me, Serena,' he whispered, and he lowered his head closer to hers.

He heard her sharp intake of breath. Satisfaction rushed through him. It didn't matter what she led him to believe—she was far from indifferent to him. For whatever reason she'd put up a barrier, and was intent on keeping him on the outside, but he wasn't going to allow that.

She placed her hand on his arm, the heat of her touch scorching him through his jacket and shirt. And as she pushed him gently back away from her she lifted her chin, bringing her lips tantalisingly close to his...

A sudden burst of applause crashed into his stirred-up senses so spectacularly he stepped back, momentarily unsure of what was happening.

Serena took in a deep breath when he drew back, as if she was surfacing from the sea. Her pulse raced wildly and the lingering scent of his spicy aftershave was doing untold things to her already unbalanced body. She'd never been so bold or so daring before. *Ever.*

She glanced up at Nikos, who seemed completely unruffled and totally composed as he turned his attention to the announcements being made. They were all in Greek, and she amused herself by observing the world Nikos inhabited. It was so far from the world she'd thought he lived in it was surreal.

Women so glamorous they might have stepped off the front of any celebrity magazine glittered with jewels. Serena found herself wondering, who, if any of these women, had been at such an event before on Nikos's arm. The array of images she'd seen on the internet that morning proved he was anything but the ordinary fisherman she'd thought he was. He was powerful, wealthy and if the array of beautiful women he'd dated was anything to go by very much a playboy.

As the speeches and applause went on Serena's mind slipped back to the first time she'd seen him. Nothing about that tanned, handsome fisherman had suggested he was anything else. But he'd been a cunning liar.

He'd smiled at her as she'd sat on the beach, enjoying the early evening sunshine, then a short time later she'd walked past the local fishing boats and had seen him again. He'd talked to her, telling her things about fishing and the local restaurants he supplied that would be useful for her article.

The attraction between them had sparked and from then on they had spent every moment they could together. Soon hot, passionate nights had followed. He'd been the man she'd been waiting for—the man she'd wanted to lose her virginity to and the man she'd thought she would be able to go on loving. She'd believed they had a future—until that last night on the beach, when his harsh words had shattered that illusion.

'Daydreaming?'

Nikos's gentle accented voice broke through her thoughts, rushing her back to the fundraising event and the glamorous reality of his life.

When she looked into his handsome face she could almost see the Nikos she'd first met and it tugged at her heartstrings. Which was the real Nikos?

'I was just wondering how you came from a small island fishing village to this.' She gestured around her at the no-expense-spared glamour of the party, at the guests moving to the sides of the room as the lights dimmed and music began.

'It's a long story,' he said, his face sombre, his eyes strangely hollow and lacking emotion.

Deep inside her she recognised pain, but before she could say anything he took her in his arms, moving them onto the dance floor as other couples began dancing around them.

She wanted to ask him more—to find out about the man she was now engaged to—but the sensation of being held close against his body as music filled the room was too much. Every move he made sent shockwaves through her and she lowered her face, keeping her eyes firmly fixed on his shoulder, not wanting him to see the flush of desire that must be evident on her cheeks.

She closed her eyes against the urge to reach up and kiss him, to indulge her fantasy of being loved by him. She couldn't let him know that was all she needed, all she wanted—not when he'd lied to her, believing she was looking only to further her career and her position in life.

The music changed, the tempo becoming faster, and she pulled back from him, thankful of the excuse to do so. The darkness of his eyes as they met hers was so consuming she drew in a sharp and ragged breath.

He took her hand in his and led her away from the bustle of dancing. Doors opened out onto a balcony, lit with an array of coloured lights that reminded her of Christmas. She glanced around to see they were alone. The music floated out on the warm evening air, and laughter could be heard, but it was just the two of them here and her heart-beat joined in with the sway of the music.

'Nikos...' she whispered, aware he was holding back from her. 'Your story—it's one I need to hear if we are going to make any kind of future together.'

A smile of satisfaction spread across his lips, drawing

her gaze briefly away from the blue of his eyes. 'So you *are* considering a future with me?'

His brittle words reminded her that they were not in love—that this was a deal, one brokered in the interest of their child. The mood changed, killing any romantic notions the dance had allowed to slip into her head.

'We are having a child, Nikos, and as much as I can't bear the idea of a marriage for that reason, or the hideous terms you've attached to it like a business deal, I don't want my child not to know his or her parents.'

She pushed thoughts of her sister aside as her mind flew back to the arguments her parents had always had. The hateful accusations they'd hurled at each other. She knew she didn't want to live like that. Worse were memories of the realisation that *she'd* forced them to stay together just by being born. She didn't ever want her child to feel that guilt. The secret love she had for the Nikos she'd first met would have to be enough—for both of them.

'Why is that a bad reason? Surely marrying for the sake of a child is best?'

'Not always, Nikos.' She smiled up at him, aware of his diverting tactics and employing some of her own. 'How did you end up here?'

What would he think if she told him about *her* childhood? Would he think that what they were doing was a mistake if she told him about how guilty she felt? She couldn't risk him turning his back on her—not when the chance to give Sally all she wanted was so tantalisingly close.

The warm wind ruffled his hair as he leant on the balcony, looking out across Athens as if it would give him answers. She moved closer to him, and the sweet fragrance of flowers around them did not quite mask the scent of his aftershave.

Without looking at her, he spoke. 'I was brought up by my grandparents and I inherited a small fleet of fishing boats when my grandfather died. I owe them a lot. They took me in when my mother left and after my father fell apart, when the truth about my mother was exposed. They gave me a start in life—which was more than either of my parents did.'

Serena remembered his insistence that he'd never wanted to be a father and her heart softened a little. The hardness of his own heart must have been caused by what he'd experienced as a child. They had both suffered due to their parents. For different reasons neither of them had seen the joy and love marriage could bring, and while she believed it might one day be possible he did not.

'But that doesn't explain how you came to be in Athens,' she said softly as she turned her back on the view and looked up at him. The soft lights highlighted his features, making his cheekbones prominent, as if they'd been chiselled from stone, hardening his expression.

'I couldn't stay on the island. It was suffocating me. So I followed an example I'd seen as a boy and left. I came here with virtually nothing but my name and began working for Dimitris, the owner of Xanthippe Shipping. He became the father I should have had.'

She frowned as she took in what he'd told her, knowing there was more buried deep inside him and knowing it was hard for him to have told her this much.

'He taught me all he knew and, without his own heir, left me his legacy. One I have built up to the global business it is today.' He turned to look down at her, his blue eyes holding her attention. 'When I first met you it was a refreshing change not to be known for my success and wealth first.'

A tang of bitterness filled her mouth. 'Did you think I

was with you for that? Or did you believe I was looking for a big break—a story that would launch me from travel writer to being the journalist I'd trained to be?'

'Both.' Suspicion and anger were woven inextricably in that one word.

His honesty stung more than lies would have done, and she pushed herself away from the balcony and moved towards the door and the sounds of the party. Behind her she heard his footsteps, felt his presence.

She didn't want to turn and see the contempt in his face—the truth of what he really thought of her. His questions about whether the baby was his now made so much more sense. As did his sudden change of mood after they'd made love that last night on the beach. Did he think she'd tricked him all along? Seduced him so brazenly she'd ensured he hadn't given contraception a thought?

She couldn't stay here any longer. She felt stifled by his pain and her love. She had to get out of here right now.

'Serena!'

Her name chased after her as she made her way into the throng of partygoers, completely oblivious to the curious stares coming her way. With her chin held high and her eyes firmly fixed on the door they'd entered earlier she walked quickly. The air was hot, the noise was too much and she needed to get out—*now*.

How had she ever thought what she felt for Nikos would be enough?

She pushed the door open and went out to the hotel lobby and on to the street. *Now* what should she do? She had no idea where she was or where she needed to go to.

Tears of frustration threatened but she took in a deep breath, forcing her shoulders to relax. As they did so large, warm hands covered them. She knew it was Nikos. Every nerve in her body tingled wildly. Nobody else did that to her.

'You can't keep running for ever, Serena,' he whispered against her hair as he pulled her back against his body, holding her close.

He obviously intended anyone watching to think their lovers' tiff was over, that passion and love had won. He wanted the scandal she threatened to be quelled and subdued.

'I didn't feel well. I needed to get out,' she said, knowing it was only half the truth.

Slowly he turned her round in his arms, giving her no alternative but to look at the firm wall of his chest or up at his face. When she did look up, what she saw made her knees weak with longing. His blue eyes were full of concern, and if she didn't know any better she'd believe it was real and not for the benefit of anyone who'd witnessed her hasty departure.

'Maybe we shouldn't discuss the past—not tonight, at least.'

His accent was heavier than ever, and his eyes reminded her of the night sky as passion swirled in them. Her heart thumped in her chest as his breathing deepened, coming faster. *This* was the man she'd fallen in love with. Handsome and passionate.

'Nikos…' she breathed as her body swayed against him. The temptation was too much in her state of heightened emotion.

His hold on her tightened as his lips met hers, tenderly stroking, forcing the fire that burned within her higher. She wound her arms around his neck, heedless of her gauzy wrap falling from her shoulders. All she cared about was being kissed by Nikos. The man she loved. The father of her child.

His lips left hers fractionally. 'We should go home,' he whispered against her lips, and she closed her eyes at the erotic sensation.

'Yes, take me home, Nikos.'

Her husky whisper ended as his lips claimed hers once more, demanding and hot. She was lost. Completely and utterly lost. Despite everything, *this* was what she wanted.

CHAPTER SEVEN

NIKOS SAT IN the back of the car, Serena's sensational body against him, and had to force himself not to touch her. Not because of the presence of the driver, but because if he did he knew he wouldn't want to stop. All he could think of right now was the privacy of his bedroom.

He watched the lights of Athens rush by, focusing on the illuminations of the Acropolis as they headed towards his apartment—anything to distract himself.

Even though his head and most definitely his heart had refused to admit it, his body had wanted Serena every night since she'd left. He'd craved her touch like a lovesick teenager, needing to feel her against him, wanting her in a way he'd never wanted any woman before.

Now she was back—and tonight he would make her his. This time, for the sake of his child, he wouldn't allow her to leave.

The car pulled up outside the apartment building and she moved away from him, across the seat and out into the night, as the doors opened. He followed her, glad to see that the reporters had moved on—probably all at the charity ball. It would be their perfect chance to get pictures of the rich and famous, and he was thankful he and Serena hadn't been noticed leaving so early.

Quickly he keyed in the number for the outside door

and, with his arm protectively around her, walked towards
the lift. She hadn't spoken since they'd left the party, but he
guessed the same desire that raged inside him was keeping her silent.

Ever since they'd first met that desire had been a powerful force to resist. It had drawn him in, making him lose all
sense of reason—and tonight was no different. He wanted
her, but he had to retain control—had to remember this
was a deal she'd agreed to. And it hadn't been because of
their baby, but because of the money to help her sister.

The lift doors opened and they walked in. The bright
lights were almost too much. Serena leant against the wall
of the lift and lowered her gaze, looking intently at the
floor. Was she trying to prevent him from seeing those
beautiful green eyes of hers? Afraid to show the burning
passion he'd felt in her as they'd danced?

'You look beautiful.'

The husky tone of his voice surprised him, and his
breath caught momentarily in his chest as she looked up
at him. The green of her eyes, almost drowned by her en-
larged pupils, made her look far sexier than he'd ever seen
her. He wanted her—more than he'd ever done.

Lust hurtled round his body as her lips parted, and he
noticed the rise and fall of her breasts, her breathing deepening.

'Thank you.'

The words were barely audible, but his body had heard
them, felt their seductive vibration caress and taunt him.

The lift doors opened but he couldn't move, his gaze
remaining locked to hers, his own breathing becoming
heavier by the second. Slowly she stood taller, straight-
ening her spine, her eyes holding his as she took one step
towards him.

'This is what it was like that last night on the beach,' she whispered, so softly he wondered if she'd actually meant him to hear. 'I couldn't fight it then either.'

'You drove me mad with desire that night,' he said, moving close enough that he could take her in his arms. But he didn't, not trusting his power of control.

His pulse throbbed with building desire, the beat thumping in his ears, and he flexed his fingers then curled them tight into his palms. He couldn't take much more of this.

Her neat brows furrowed slightly and questions raced across her face. 'It was our last night. It should have been goodbye.'

The lift doors closed, breaking the spell that had woven inextricably around them. Serena looked away, almost flustered by what had just happened, and frustration gave way to irritation as he pressed the button to open the doors again.

Whatever had been started that night on the beach in Santorini was far from over. He didn't appreciate the hold she had over him, the way she could make him want her just with a glance or a whispered word, but he couldn't ignore it any longer.

He stepped out of the lift and turned to see her watching him. 'I want you, Serena.'

He couldn't explain why he'd said it, why he'd exposed his emotions. He pressed his lips firmly together to avoid saying anything else he might regret—something she might later use against him. He *did* want her—of that there wasn't any doubt—but that didn't mean he had to bring emotions into it. That was something he could never do…especially when she was here for her own reasons.

She stepped towards him, her long legs outlined through the pale silk of the dress, causing the blood to pound harder around his heated body and his thoughts to spiral away to nothing.

'I want you too.'

The tremulous whisper, so timid and quiet, made him grit his teeth together. She deserved better than him. She deserved a man who would love her—one who would be what she needed him to be. But fate had intervened and, as much as he desired her, he didn't know if he could be that man. His past had shaped him to an emotionally cold man who would never be able to love a woman with real sincerity, but inside he still burned with desire for her.

Serena saw his jaw clench and knew she shouldn't have said anything. She shouldn't have told him she wanted him, giving him power over her once more. Such thoughts made everything impossible.

She couldn't take a single step towards him, and stayed inside the lift as he stepped out.

Nikos had proposed to her, bought her the most gorgeous engagement ring—not only out of duty, but because of the deal they'd made. It was pure blackmail, but it would enable her sister to become a mother. Her spirits dropped at the thought that none of it would have happened if their night together hadn't resulted in consequences.

As the assistant in the jeweller's had spoken of lovers being brought closer by emeralds her heart had flickered with a little flame of hope. He'd taken the ring and purposefully put it on her finger, but she knew he hadn't given it because of love. Deep down, she knew he didn't love her and never would. He only wanted his child and he was prepared to offer anything.

She looked at Nikos, resplendent in his evening suit, so handsome he took her breath away. As his gaze met hers, full of desire, she saw the man she'd fallen in love with—the one she'd thought she knew so well. His gaze lingered on her, and despite the trappings of wealth and power the fisherman who'd stolen her heart was still there. Deep beneath the surface, but still there.

The flicker of hope that something could be salvaged grew.

The doors of the lift began to close again, startling her, and with lightning-quick reaction Nikos moved forward, stopping the doors. He held out his hand to her, his face serious and intent. If she took his hand now it would mean so much more than this moment. She would be accepting everything.

Her heart beat a loud rhythm as she looked into his eyes, searching for answers to questions she dared not ask. He didn't move, didn't break eye contact as a myriad of thoughts crashed over her. Finally she did what she knew she had to, what she knew was inevitable, and placed her hand in his.

He braced his body against the lift doors as they threatened to close again and closed his hand around hers. His blue eyes continued to lure her as she walked towards him, and with her hand tightly in his, her body sizzling from his touch, they walked out of the lift and towards his apartment.

The key turning in the lock made a loud click, highlighting the laden silence. With purpose he opened the door, leading her through and then pushing it swiftly shut behind him. Before she could say anything his body pressed her against the wall of the hallway, his hands against the wall on either side of her head. His lips claimed hers in a deep and demanding kiss and she arched herself against him, winding her arms about his neck.

This was what she'd wanted for the past three months. As the magnitude of her pregnancy had registered, shocking her with its implications, she'd still wanted him. Even the shocking deal he'd put to her hadn't dampened the passion in any way, and right now all she wanted was to love him—enough for both of them.

'Serena…' he whispered as he pulled back from her, his fingers tangling in her hair. 'With passion such as this burning between us it doesn't matter why we are together. The marriage *will* work.'

Her heart broke a little. But what had she expected? Words of love? In reality she knew she'd never hear such words from Nikos. He didn't want to love or be loved, but he was right about the passion. It sparked between them like fireworks on New Year's Eve. It was wild and reckless and totally consuming.

'Yes—yes, it will.' She stumbled over the words, her breath coming in short gasps. She couldn't completely take in what he'd said. Her body trembled too much with need for his touch.

He lowered his head, pressing his lips so gently against hers she almost cried. Then he traced a line of soft kisses down her neck, lingering on her shoulder as she tilted her head to one side, allowing him greater access and sighing with pleasure. The fingers entwined in her hair pulled free and stroked her cheek tenderly.

She reached up, placing her hand over his, stilling the movement. It was too much. It made her dare to believe he loved her. But she knew he didn't. She knew it was nothing more than lust.

He looked into her eyes and smiled, the lips that had just kissed her neck so persuasively drawing her gaze.

'I will make you mine, Serena, and the only place for that is in my bed.'

She couldn't fight him any longer. Being in his arms, his bed—it was all she wanted, all her body craved.

'Then take me there,' she teased, shocking herself, but enjoying the sexy look Nikos gave her. Would it be so bad to give in to what raged between them when they were to be married?

He stood back from her, his heavy gaze sweeping down her body, lingering on her breasts for just long enough to send heat hurtling through her. Again he took her hand and led her through the apartment to the only room she hadn't yet seen. His bedroom.

He opened the door, revealing a masculine space dominated by a large bed, bathed in the glow of golden light coming through the balcony windows.

He drew her into the room and looked down at her. Slowly he pulled his tie undone, tossing it to the floor, where it was soon joined by his jacket. She looked at the shirt, so white against his dark skin, and willed her eyes to stay open instead of closing in pleasure.

She remembered how his chest felt. How the hair there enabled her fingers to glide across his muscles. But most of all she remembered the firmness, and she ached to touch him again. She reached out and spread her fingers over his chest, relishing the feel of his arms pulling her to him, holding her there.

'I need you,' she said softly, not daring to look into his face in case her love shone out.

Instead she concentrated on opening one button of his shirt, then, when she didn't meet any resistance, another and another, until she could slide her hand inside. The groan of pleasure escaping him encouraged her further.

His fingers struggled briefly with the zip on her dress and she stifled a nervous laugh.

'I want to see you,' he said hoarsely. 'I want to see all of you.'

Seconds later the bodice of her dress loosened as he unzipped it, and then the pale green silk slithered down, leaving her naked apart from her panties and dainty sandals.

She resisted the urge to cover herself with her arms. She'd never stood so blatantly naked before him, always shielding herself from his gaze, anxious because of her innocence. It took great effort to remain under the scrutiny of those sexy blue eyes without covering herself as they devoured her hungrily.

A guttural growl of Greek words rushed from him as his gaze lingered on her. Before she could ask what he'd said his fingers caressed a blazing trail down her arms, stroking all the way to her hands, then her fingertips. He lightly lifted her fingers and brought each in turn to his lips and kissed them, and all the while his gaze, heady and deep blue, held her face, making her blush with desire.

'You are a goddess,' he said, kissing along one arm until he came to her shoulder.

Her whole body was on fire, her breasts tender and full, yearning for his touch. But still he kissed her shoulder, teasing and tormenting her as she'd never known before. Then slowly the fiery trail of kisses moved downwards and she gasped in pleasure, hardly able to stand.

'A goddess who is all mine,' he said huskily, and each word was interspersed with kisses, pressed enticingly against her, moving down between her breasts until she ached for him to kiss them.

His head moved lower, his kisses now on the soft swell of her stomach, and she plunged her fingers into his hair, closing her eyes.

'Nikos…' His name rushed from her lips on a wave of pleasure and she pressed them tightly together in case she said more.

'Such a beautiful body.'

His kisses moved down over her stomach, lingering as his hands skimmed her bottom, the sensation almost unbalancing her. She felt his warm breath against the silky panties that left little to the imagination and fought hard to remain standing.

Just when she thought she might collapse onto the bed behind her his fingers trailed down her thighs and towards her ankles.

'I intend to savour every part of it.'

Nikos looked up at Serena, her face so flushed with desire. The blood pounded harder around his body. He took a deep breath, fighting to regain some kind of control. He wanted to push her onto the white covers of the bed and lose himself inside her until the madness she evoked stopped—but he couldn't. This time he had to take it slow, had to keep a tight rein on the desire that burned inside him, because this was different from any other time.

He didn't known how or why. All he knew was that this was the woman he was going to marry, the mother of his child, a woman who'd unlocked something deep inside him that he couldn't yet acknowledge. From the moment he'd met her she'd changed him somehow, but he couldn't analyse it now.

Whatever it was it had the potential to be painful, the capability to be render him helpless, just like the hurt that had crushed him as a boy, and he never wanted to put himself in the firing line of that kind of pain again.

He stood up and looked down into her face, saw the nervousness in her eyes and felt as if his chest was being squeezed. 'This is what you want?'

Her big green eyes blinked rapidly, then she smiled up at him and his heart seemed to stop.

'Yes,' she whispered softly, tilting her chin and pressing her lips against his in a tormenting and lingering kiss. 'Yes, it is. I want you, Nikos.'

He pulled her against him, wishing he wasn't still

clothed so that he could feel her soft skin against his. A groan of desire escaped him as her feather-light kisses teased his senses, pushing him to the edge of his control.

He took her face between his hands, holding her at just the right angle, and kissed her until she murmured against his lips. Then he slid his tongue between them, deepening the kiss.

He closed his eyes against the exquisite pain of having her all but naked in his arms and having to exert control, trying to consider her condition. It was torture. He could feel her hardened nipples pressing against his chest, with only his partially open shirt between them, and as she wound her arms around his neck, pulling her body closer still, he had to hold back the urge to allow his desire to get the better of him.

He let go of her face, kissing her harder and deeper. His hands skimmed down the curve of her back, making her arch even closer, then he held her, pressing her against him. It wasn't enough. He wanted more—much more.

He grasped her thighs, lifting her off the floor until she wrapped her legs about him. Her fingers tangled in his hair as she kissed him deeply, her sighs of pleasure rushing into him, entwining with his. Slowly he walked the few paces to the bed and, with a steadiness that tested all his strength, lowered her onto the white covers. Then he hooked his fingers inside her panties and pulled them down, not taking his gaze from her face as she smiled seductively at him, passion making her uninhibited.

The golden glow from outside was the only light in the room. Every curve of her delicious body was bathed in soft amber and he inhaled deeply, trying to keep his rush of lust under control.

She slithered up the bed, away from him, but he caught

her ankle in a firm grip that made the breath rush from her lips.

'Now these,' he said, and unfastened the tiny straps of her sandals, inwardly cursing as his fingers fumbled with the delicate buckles.

She propped herself up on her arms and watched him. As he dropped the second glittering sandal to the floor she reached for him. He knelt on the bed, his body over hers, and kissed her, wishing he could touch her, but his arms had locked, supporting his weight. He didn't want to hurt her.

Her heated kisses became frantic, her breath fast, as her fingers continued what they'd started earlier and she opened his shirt, pushing it over his shoulders. He shook with the effort of restraining his control.

She kissed down his neck, over his shoulder, her hands tugging at his shirt until it was tight around his arms. He pushed back so that he straddled her legs, almost ripping the shirt off, and was rewarded with the darkening of her eyes until they were like the heart of a forest on a moon-lit night.

'How did I ever think I wanted to let you go?'

As he said the words her fingers traced the line of hair down over his abs, making breathing almost impossible. She lingered at the fastening of his trousers, the smile on her lips telling him she knew exactly the effect she was having on him.

'Do you really feel that?' she whispered, her fingers teasing as they travelled up and down the line of dark hair. But she refused to meet his eyes, shielding her face from him with a curtain of glorious amber hair.

'Yes,' he growled harshly, his lips claiming hers as he pushed her back against the bed.

If he said any more now he would be going into emotions he didn't want to explore—feelings he didn't want to admit to, let alone experience.

Her hands moved to rest on his thighs, inflicting yet more torture.

Serena's heart raced. He hadn't wanted to let her go. Did that mean he felt something for her? Even if it wasn't love?

She kissed him hard, demanding more from him as his body forced her to lie back against the bed. Her fingers tightened on his strong thighs and his groan of pleasure exploded into her mouth.

He wanted her—*really* wanted her. All her naivety and innocence had been left behind as she'd entered the apartment. She was his and his alone.

'Nikos…' It was all she could say, her breathing deep and ragged. But she wanted to tell him she was back and that she would never go. They were bound together by their baby, and maybe with passion such as this burning between them he would one day love her.

'This is too much. You tease and taunt me, pushing me beyond my control.'

He caught her hands in his, holding them against his thighs, preventing her teasing. His face was stern, his eyes so dark that only blue flecks remained.

With a swift suddenness he moved off her, springing to stand by the bed, removing the last of his clothes, tossing them carelessly away. Her heart pumped ever harder and she couldn't drag her gaze from his magnificent body. Her fingers itched to touch him, to caress every part of him, but most of all to feel him against her, then inside her, making her completely his.

The need she had for him was like nothing she'd ever known. Feeling brazen and emboldened, she looked at his naked and aroused body. 'No more teasing,' she said in a broken whisper as heat gathered low in her stomach. If he didn't make love to her soon she'd go insane.

'No,' he said huskily as he lay on the bed next to her, and the command in his voice was palpable. 'Not from you at least.'

Her eyes closed and a sigh of pleasure escaped her as he bent his head, kissing her nipple and sending shockwaves of pure pleasure through her. She arched her back, lifting herself higher as he nipped gently at it, but when his hand rested on her stomach she almost didn't dare breathe. After a moment's pause he slowly moved it lower, exploring the part of her that wanted him with a fiery heat that refused to be put out.

'It's my turn,' he said as he raised his head, her nipple tingling from his kisses.

He turned his attention to the other one as his fingers caressed her, stoking the fire of passion almost to breaking point. She gripped his arm, wanting him to stop, wanting her moment of ecstasy to be shared with his.

'No, Nikos!'

'Yes,' he said against her breast, exerting more of his power over her, and she dug her fingers harder into his arm.

Just when she thought he'd gone too far he stopped the torment and moved over her, his knees nudging her legs apart as he kissed her deeply, bruising her lips with the intensity of his kiss. She felt the heat of him against her and lifted her hips, begging him with her body for release.

Gently he slid into her, bringing tears to her eyes, and she wondered if he was restraining himself, holding back because of the baby. Instinctively she wrapped her legs around him, pulling him deeper into her. His arms, braced tightly to keep his weight off her, began to shake with the effort and she kissed his chest, his neck, his chin until they both lost control.

Nikos kissed her back, interspersing his kisses with Greek words she had no hope of understanding, but it didn't matter. Her mind was floating too much even to even form the question and ask what he'd said. Maybe it was better if she didn't. Maybe she should pretend they were words of love…feed her fantasy of a happy-ever-after.

As she moved beneath him she realised it had never been like this before. The wild passion they shared had never tipped her so far over the edge. She clung to him, not wanting the moment to end.

Finally her breathing slowed and he lowered himself over her, propped on his elbows, but his heated skin was still touching hers, sending a tingle of pleasure all over her.

He dropped his head against her shoulder, his thick dark hair tickling her cheek. 'You will not leave again.'

The words were muffled, his voice hoarse and uneven, but she couldn't miss the aggressive harshness in it. There was no mistaking its dominance and power. The fairy tale was over.

She closed her eyes and cried inside. He was still angry. Did he even now resent having her in his life? Resent the baby they'd created in the summer? Was she right to have come back? Was she right to have accepted his offer to help Sally, tying herself and her baby to him for ever?

CHAPTER EIGHT

THE SUN WAS streaming in through the windows when Nikos woke the next morning, shocking him. He *never* slept late. He moved and a sigh of contentment from Serena stirred his senses—along with memories from last night. He'd made love to her until exhaustion had claimed them both. No wonder he hadn't woken at his usual early hour.

'Morning.'

Serena's husky voice caught his attention and he looked down at her as she moved against him, unwittingly enticing him once more.

Never before had he woken with a woman in his bed. He'd always slipped from *their* beds, early in the morning, preferring not to get into those *what happens next?* discussions. Leaving them sleeping had always given a clear message. Just as never taking a woman to his own bed served as a constant reminder why he shouldn't get involved in long-term affairs.

So why had he felt the need to bring Serena here when she'd offered to check into a hotel? Was it just because he was going to marry her? Or was it more than the need to keep her in his life now that she was carrying his child?

He pushed the suggestion firmly from his mind and inwardly cursed his train of thought. What was the matter with him? He'd never agonised over spending the night with a woman before.

'Are you rested enough to go out today?' He asked the question as he moved away from the temptation of her lush curves, throwing back the covers and walking naked to the bathroom.

He splashed cold water over his face in an attempt to cool his returning ardour, as well as shock the heavy combination of sleep and passion from his body. An icy shower was what he needed most. And as the cold jets of water pounded his skin he thought back to every minute of last night, to the way Serena had made him feel.

His desire had not been for her alone, but for things he shouldn't want. From the very first night they'd spent together she'd made him want more, and each time that need filtered through his mind just a little more clearly. But he couldn't allow it. He would not let himself feel anything other than passion for any woman—especially not Serena. If he did it was sure to spell disaster. Hadn't his past proved he was incapable of loving or being loved?

With an unsettled feeling he switched off the shower, towelled his hair dry and then slung a white towel around his hips and returned to the bedroom. Serena was still in bed, half asleep and looking as lovely as ever, her red hair not in its usual sleek style, but ruffled from a night of making love.

'I thought you would be going to the office,' she said softly, pushing her tumbled hair from her eyes and sitting up, pulling the white sheet against her, looking suddenly vulnerable.

As he watched her it was as if someone had notched something tight around his chest, but he smiled at her modesty, tempted to remind her that last night she hadn't cared if he saw her body.

'Not today.'

'What about your deal? I thought it was getting close to completion?'

She curled her legs underneath her and knelt on the bed, moving the sheet, giving him a glimpse of her thighs.

'It's Saturday, and we need to be seen out together.'

He knew what she'd meant, and it had nothing to do with their deal. After each night they'd stayed together in her hotel room in Santorini he'd slipped away as dawn had broken, his job—which she'd believed was fishing— being the perfect reason and therefore not requiring any justification.

'There is nothing more to be done with that deal until Monday.'

Unlike the deal he'd struck with Serena.

She smiled and something tugged hard on his guilt. She really did deserve a man who could love her—but he could never be that man. He didn't want the experience of watching someone leave again, her cruel words haunting him ever since.

'If we must go out, I'd like to go to the Acropolis.'

Her excitement cast a glow over her face and he realised she looked the happiest he'd seen her since she'd returned to Greece. For the first time since her text had come through the thought came that things could work out between them. Providing she didn't ask for that one thing he couldn't give—emotional commitment.

'Then I suggest you get dressed.'

He turned and selected clothes from his wardrobe, dropping the towel with scant regard for his nakedness. Behind him, he heard her intake of breath and smiled. The passion of last night still simmered within her, just as it did for him, and if he didn't get out of the bedroom now he was in danger of spending all day in bed—and that was something for lovers to do.

Serena felt as if her whole body glowed as she and Nikos walked along the path towards the Acropolis. The sun was hot, but her memories of last night were hotter, and now, with her hand in his, she felt the fizz of passion brewing again, along with the warm glow of hope. Last night had been just like when they'd first met. It had proved the heated passion that they had always shared was still there—but was it enough?

Around them crowds of tourists posed for photos and admired the view over the rooftops of Athens. Children squealed in delight as they clambered over the many rocks and Serena watched them, the reality of her situation coming to her clearly. This was her child's history, and by staying and marrying Nikos she would give her sister the same chance of motherhood she now had.

A pang of guilt slid over her.

'Are we doing the right thing?' She looked out at the view, not daring to look at him. His hand around hers tightened, but he continued to walk.

'How can we *not* be doing the right thing, Serena?'

His words were firm and quiet as he guided her towards some meagre shade, out of the way of a large tour party noisily heading towards them.

She looked up at him, glad of the shade, and waited until the tourists had passed, with their enthusiasm and animated exclamations of delight.

'I find it hard to believe a man like you hasn't married.'

His dark brows arched, and she wasn't sure if it was the shade of the trees or what she'd said that had given his face those stern and sharp lines.

'A man like me?' He let her hand go and thrust it into the pocket of his casual beige chinos, his stance suddenly annoyed, his expression confrontational.

'You have it all, Nikos. Surely women have been throwing themselves at you, looking for marriage? So why me? Why now?' She pushed on, determined to clear the doubts that had begun to surface since she'd arrived, only to be pushed aside last night by passion. But as that passion had cooled those doubts had slipped back into her mind—like snakes slithering undetected through the long grass.

'Why?' His deep voice was harsh, causing a passing tourist to glance their way, and Nikos took her arm and walked her further away from the path and the crowds. He stopped and turned to look at her. 'Do you really need to ask that?'

She drew in a deep breath, lifted her chin and met his glittering blue gaze. 'Yes.'

She *did* need to ask. She needed to know if there was even an inkling of love there for her. Sally's advice was fading fast as the reality of the deal he'd offered sank in. She didn't think she could go headlong into marriage without knowing he felt *some* kind of affection for her. What if he later resented her, when he couldn't attend parties like last night's as a single man? What if he fell in love with another woman?

'You are carrying my child. My heir.'

Fury spiked every word but she stood her ground. She had to know.

'Nothing else?' She pressed him further, ignoring the glitter of anger in his eyes.

'Is that not reason enough?'

He turned away from her, looking out over Athens towards Mount Lycabettus and St George's chapel reaching into the blue sky. His anger was in complete contrast to the sublime weather.

She moved to stand by him, her flat shoes crunching on the path, the sound so loud it was almost too much in the heavy and expectant silence which had settled around them.

'Is it right for us to marry just because of the baby? What about the baby's feelings? Should it grow up thinking it's the mistake that forced us together?'

The pain and guilt of her own childhood poured from her heart, seeping into every word she said, but still he remained ramrod-straight, looking anywhere but at her. A small part of her wanted to tell him she knew what that was like, but lifelong guilt kept her silent. She couldn't admit her part in her parents' unhappy marriage—not out loud.

'What do you want me to do? Declare my undying love for you?' His voice was low, vibrating with anger. 'You accepted my terms. You need this marriage and all it offers as much as I do.'

She balked at his mention of the deal he'd offered—the one she was prepared to take if it meant helping Sally get what she wanted. She still hadn't told her sister yet. The thought of ringing her and telling her she could continue with IVF treatment was exciting, but explaining how it was going to be achieved was daunting. As was telling Sally of her own pregnancy. It was a conversation to be had face-to-face.

'We can't build a marriage on a child and a foundation of lust. What happens when that lust dies?'

She forced her voice to be strong and wished they weren't surrounded by people of all nationalities, that this discussion was taking place in private—but maybe the restraint of being here was better.

He turned to look at her, his hands taking hold of her

arms, forcing her to give him all her attention. Her skin burned where he touched her and a sizzle of undeniable attraction skittered down her spine. How could she find such a ruthless man so attractive?

'Love dies too, Serena.'

His deep, accented words, said with such earnestness, forced her to search his eyes. They looked so black and solemn that a tingle of fear chased after the sizzle of attraction she'd tried so hard to ignore. The sombre tones of his voice left her in no doubt that he was talking from experience.

'What happened?' She wanted to reach for him, to soothe the pain which lingered in his eyes like dark shadows in the night.

He didn't say anything, and nor did he break eye contact. Even when a particularly noisy party of tourists started posing for photos with Mount Lycabettus as a backdrop, intruding on their private moment, he remained rigidly silent.

He waited, and she hardly dared to breathe, sensing that the impenetrable barrier around him had opened just enough for her to slip through—if she dared.

'You'll find it on the internet, I'm sure.'

The spiked and curt words reminded her of the expression of regret she'd seen on his face yesterday, when he'd arrived from the office to find her working on her laptop. She hadn't been searching for stories of him then, but knew that was what it must have looked like. What was in his past that was so bad? What was he avoiding?

Something akin to fear gripped her heart and she had to hear it from him. 'I want *you* to tell me.' Her voice was a whisper, but a firm and decisive one. He'd said this much and she couldn't let him shut down on her now.

He let go of her and turned to stand looking out at the

view. His profile was set in stern lines, but she moved towards him, her body so close to his they were almost touching. Almost.

'I'd been here in Athens for two years and had put my every waking hour into Xanthippe Shipping. I'd made the money I wanted and more. Everything finally seemed to be going right—until my mother wrote to me.'

'I don't understand,' she said softly, placing her hand on his arm.

He looked at her, his fierce blue eyes a total contrast to the way he'd just spoken. '*Don't* you?'

The question hurt. It was prodding, as if to try and revive a dying flame. Memories of a childhood that had made her push men away as a young woman, wary of being hurt, rushed towards her in a stampede.

She shook her head.

'No, of course you don't. *You* had the happy home every child deserves.' His brow furrowed.

He was too close now to her upsetting childhood, and her heart thumped so hard it blocked out the hum of tourists talking and laughing. There was no way she could tell him the truth. How could she say she'd loved him from the moment they met when he thought she'd only returned for financial gain? Hadn't she confirmed his suspicions by accepting his offer to fund more IVF for Sally—accepting his marriage deal?

'You don't know anything about me,' she whispered in a half-truth, desperate to look away from the accusation in his eyes but not daring to. 'And that's changing the subject. What happened, Nikos?'

She saw his jaw clench, the hard lines highlighting his cheekbones, his eyes hard and suspicious. 'My mother's *"love"* died when she found someone with more wealth, more able to give her all she wanted. She left me with my father. He didn't care about my pain—just drank himself into oblivion.'

The harsh way he'd all but snarled the word *love* was not lost on her and she drew in a ragged breath, moving away from him, away from his contempt of the emotion she felt so strongly for him.

Nikos stood looking at the view of St George's chapel. The sun was bouncing off its white walls as it sat perched on top of the tree-lined mountain opposite. This was supposed to be a day out. A time for Serena to see a place she'd expressed an interest in—a place that was part of his child's legacy. Instead it had turned to deep and unwelcome exploration of his past.

He sensed Serena by his side, the heat of her body reminding him of the passion they'd shared last night. That passion would be the foundation for their marriage. Serena had shown her true self in accepting his deal. She would do whatever it took to get what she wanted. Love hadn't been a part of what they'd shared those few weeks on Santorini, and it certainly wouldn't be a part of their marriage. Lust was all he could offer—because he couldn't give more. Not ever.

'My mother walked away without a backward glance.' He said the words aloud, not realising he had done so until he felt Serena move at his side. He looked down at her. 'We are better off marrying for our convenience—and for the baby, Serena. Emotions are messy and complicated things.'

He'd wondered initially at Serena's motives when she'd returned—had been sure that she'd discovered his true identity, that she was looking for whatever it was his mother had found in the man she'd left his father for. That fear hadn't dissipated. Still doubts niggled. But one thing was certain. He could not and would not be a victim of love again. He'd care for Serena in every way possible, but never again did he want to expose himself to such rejection, such heartache.

Nothing else in his life compared to the pain he'd carried since the day his mother had left. Her words still haunted him, killing any of the attempts to make amends she'd made over the years.

Serena moved away from him, walking among the scattered stones as they lay in the parched earth and for a moment he couldn't move. Then she turned and smiled so bright he wondered if he had imagined all they'd just spoken about.

She held out her hand to him. 'There is more to see?'

He was grateful for the change in subject and, slamming the door of his past shut, he walked over and took her hand.

The wonder on her face as she walked towards the Parthenon a short time later held his vulnerable emotions captive. He watched as she reached out and touched the cream stone that had been there for thousands of years, and despite their earlier conversation he was glad he'd chosen to spend the day with her.

The two weeks they'd spent together on Santorini came back to him. Nothing else had mattered. He'd lived those two weeks only for each moment, for each smile from her adorable lips, each kiss which had set light to him, and each gentle and alluringly innocent touch.

It had been like looking in on the life he could have had—but they would never find that again. No, those two weeks now meant he was to be a father.

The thought filled him with wonder and dread.

As the sun grew higher in the sky Serena looked weary. She still smiled, still wanted to know all he could tell her about the ancient temple, but she was looking hot and tired. Concern for her and for the baby filled him.

'We should go now.' He looked at his watch, surprised that they had been out so long. The appointment he'd arranged with a doctor before leaving Santorini was in just an hour. 'The doctor is calling later.'

'Doctor?' She blinked in confusion and fixed him with those green eyes. 'On a Saturday? I don't need to see a doctor that urgently.'

'Maybe not, but you will. It has all been arranged.'

He took her hand, but sensed her hesitation as they began to walk back through the mass of tourists. At least they would have some time alone at the apartment. His body heated at the memory of their last hours alone together.

'Do you still doubt you are the father?'

He turned to her instantly, to see that she was looking at the ground, as if concentrating on every step instead of meeting his gaze.

'In the past two days you have flown across Europe alone and then travelled here to Athens. You admitted you were ill for the first months of your pregnancy. You *will* see a doctor. I do not want my child being put at risk.'

She stopped and looked at him. Hostility and disbelief were burning in her eyes, but she didn't say anything. Before he could rein in his frustration at knowing she'd spent those months alone and ill, unable to tell anyone, she began walking again—but this time with purposeful strides which clearly displayed her annoyance.

Serena answered all the questions the Greek doctor put to her, aware of Nikos's brooding presence behind her. He didn't trust her. That much was evident. But was it because he didn't believe the child was his or because he genuinely cared about it?

As the doctor spoke in Greek over her, ignoring her, her temper simmered. Nikos didn't care—not about her. All he cared about was making sure the baby was his. How had she been so stupid as to think that the hours they'd spent making love last night would make him see her differently?

She couldn't sit here and allow them to talk about her like this. It was, after all, *her* baby they were talking about.

'What is he saying?' she asked a little too firmly, her irritation directed at Nikos, not the older man.

'That you need to rest and must take things easy.' He looked at her, his eyes glittering like the sea had done on that day they'd first met, as if sprinkled with diamonds.

'Yes—rest,' added the doctor in heavily accented English as he made his way towards the door. 'The nausea will subside and you will feel well again soon.'

She smiled her thanks at him, wondering how she could ever 'feel well again', knowing the man she loved would never love her.

'Thank you. Sorry to have troubled you.'

'Nothing is too much trouble for Nikos. He was like a son to my cousin and he made him very happy.'

She frowned at his words as Nikos shut the door after the doctor and returned to the living room. 'Who is his cousin?'

'His cousin was the man I worked for when I first came to Athens—the man I looked up to and the man who was more of a father to me than my own.'

'Do you ever see your father and mother?'

As he looked at her she saw his eyes dim, as if a shutter had been drawn down over them.

'My father died when I was a teenager, but I hadn't really known him since my mother left. It destroyed him, changed him. I went to live with my grandparents.'

Serena's heart went out to him as she imagined what he must have felt. Her parents had constantly squabbled, and her home had sometimes felt unsettled as divorce threats were bandied about like a ball on the tennis court, but they had always been in her life.

'What about your grandmother? Do you see her?' she asked, remembering the woman he'd said lived in the small white house, perched on the hillside overlooking the sea.

'She took me in and raised me—gave me everything she could,' he said gruffly. 'I returned that care when my grandfather died and at her insistence I kept his small fleet of fishing boats.'

'That is why you were helping with the fishing when we met? When you couldn't tell me the truth?'

Things were starting to fit together now, but it still didn't explain his need to strike such a deal with her.

He nodded and walked to the balcony, but she wasn't going to be knocked off course so easily.

'Will your grandmother approve?'

Serena wondered about what the old lady would think of him taking an English bride—and a pregnant one at that. What would she think of the terms of their marriage?

'She is a very wise lady.' He looked down at her where she sat. 'She would also tell you to rest, to look after yourself and the baby.'

Serena placed her hand over her stomach and looked into Nikos's eyes, her heart somersaulting at the swirling desire she saw in them once more, and found herself longing for this evening. Would he take her to his bed again? Make love to her gently and yet so passionately? She knew she shouldn't want that, but she did. She couldn't just switch her love off—or her hope that one day he might love her.

'Does she know about the baby?'

He shook his head and she couldn't help voicing her concern.

'Because you doubt the baby is yours?'

There—she'd said the words aloud, cast them out like a fisherman's net, giving him the chance to agree, to call a halt to everything.

He didn't. He merely looked at her. A long, cold stare that made her want to shiver, as if winter winds were suddenly being blown in off the sea.

'I have never doubted the baby is mine, Serena,' he said as he sat down next to her. 'But I do doubt that you are looking after yourself. You should not have flown all the way here alone. You should have called me from London— as soon as you knew. As I asked you to.'

'What could you have done—or what could the man I *thought* you were have done? *He* wouldn't have been able to arrange for a private plane to fly him to England.' Hurt smarted inside her as she remembered his deceit, but maybe after their brief talk today the reason was a little clearer.

He stepped closer, leaned down and kissed her softly on the lips, his dark mood thawing as passion took over the blue of his eyes. 'It doesn't matter who you thought I was when we were together. I've told you—I didn't want to spoil our time with each other, a time that was special. Different.'

She searched his face and placed her palm against his cheek, feeling a fresh growth of stubble, but she knew that the special time they'd shared during the summer was over. Reality had impinged on it.

'You could have told me the truth.'

His answer was to pull her into his arms and kiss her, engulfing them both in a desire that would have only one outcome. She kissed him back, hoping the love she had for him, a love he would never want, would be enough—for her *and* their marriage.

CHAPTER NINE

NIKOS WAS SURPRISED by the ease with which he had slipped into sharing his life with Serena. Each morning for the past week he'd kissed her goodbye, tearing himself from her warm body to go to the office. He'd been pleased that she'd taken the doctor's advice and was resting, and each day she looked more radiant and more vibrant, which was having an uncontrollable effect on him.

He thought it was what a real relationship might be like, and that was something he'd become an expert at avoiding. But two weeks with Serena in the summer and one intensely passionate night had changed his life, forcing him to look his worst fears in the eye. Fear of failure and an even bigger fear of love.

This morning the deal he'd been working on had finally gone through. He was now the owner of the largest shipping company in Greece, with both cargo ships *and* cruise liners that would sail the seas under his name. He'd achieved his ambition. Now it was time to seal a different deal—one that would bind Serena to him for ever.

But before he could do that he had to visit his grandmother on Santorini. He couldn't put it off any longer, and hoped the news of their engagement and the baby didn't reach her before he did. His conscience unsettled by such thoughts, he'd ordered his plane and was now flying across a glittering sea littered with islands.

A soft sigh from Serena drew his attention back from the view and he looked across at her. Even though the afternoon flight was short, she'd fallen asleep almost immediately. A little spike of guilt caught him unawares. Had their passion-filled nights tired her too much?

She opened her eyes, sat up and looked at him, the smile on her lips making him want to lean across and kiss her. But the crew who manned his private plane were now preparing for landing. He would have to wait until they were alone at his villa this evening.

'We will be there soon,' he said, and put the papers he had hardly looked at away, having preferred instead to watch Serena while she was sleeping.

He still couldn't comprehend that he'd spent a week enjoying coming home to her each day, savouring the nights with her sleeping in his arms. He'd been stunned when he'd realised that he now lingered in the mornings, not wanting to leave her. He hadn't ever done that with any other woman. Even when he and Serena had shared nights of passionate sex whilst she was staying in the hotel when they'd first met he'd slipped from her bed as the sun rose.

So what had changed?

She now wore his ring, making his intention to marry her clear to everyone. But why, after locking his heart away, was he even considering marriage? Deep down he knew it was more than just the fact that she was carrying his child, his heir, but he didn't want to look beyond that right now—was worried that if he searched too hard for answers it would all be destroyed, that history would repeat itself and he'd be declared unworthy of love or affection.

He narrowed his eyes as a new thought slipped insidiously through his mind, pushing aside the need to question his motives. She'd come back because of the baby, declaring she had no intention of staying. Would she have come back, contacted him again, if it hadn't been for his warning that night on the beach? She'd walked away from him then. Had she meant it to be for good?

He relaxed as the answer came to him like a bolt of lightning. She had come back because she had known all along who he was—had known of his wealth and had come to get what she wanted. Money for her sister.

'Nikos…?'

His name, softly spoken, with a question in it, dragged him from his black thoughts.

'Is something wrong?'

'No.' He forced a smile to his lips and pushed away the shadows of doubt, returning to his first thoughts. 'I just hope my grandmother hasn't heard our news second hand.'

'Is that likely?'

A worried frown creased her brow and her eyes looked so soft they reminded him of the deep green of the sea on calm days, when he stopped his boat to cast the nets.

He thought of the headlines their engagement had made, coupled with the deal he'd successfully completed. It would be a miracle if his grandmother *didn't* know. What would she think of him taking an English bride after everything his mother had put the family through?

'I think it is. She may live in a small village, but others will have told her.'

It was far better that Serena was prepared. His grandmother was a wise and canny lady, who wouldn't appreciate being outsmarted.

He thought of the basic house she lived in—more of a tourist attraction than a home—and wished his grandmother had been less stubborn and moved into the villa he'd built for her on the island. She'd refused completely, and after several years of it being empty he'd decided to use it as his base when he was back on the island. Whenever he returned there his grandmother always knew, so why should knowledge of his engagement be any different?

Nikos didn't want to tell Serena that news travelled fast the other way too—that he'd known of her arrival on the island before she'd sent him that text. She'd been asking for him, and his friends had told her he'd gone away for a while, but let him know she was there. It still hadn't prepared him for seeing those words boldly glaring up at him from his phone, for knowing that the consequences he'd least wanted had happened.

She looked dismayed, and he pushed aside his unease to allay hers. 'It will be fine. If anyone is to blame it is me. I should have told her.'

Serena took Nikos's hand as they climbed the twists and turns of the steps to the little white house almost at the top of the hill. She was totally charmed by all the houses, which appeared to be clinging to the hillside. Most were white, reflecting the heat of the sun and making sunglasses necessary, but others were pale pink or cream, and some had the blue-painted domed roofs typical of the region.

'How do people *live* here?' She laughed as she paused to rest on a flat area that seemed suspended above the houses below, their roofs like steps back down to the sea.

'You get used to it.' He looked at her with genuine concern, despite his light-hearted response. 'Are you feeling okay?'

'I'm fine.' She laughed again. 'I just wanted to stop and take in the view.'

She turned and looked out to the sparkling sea and felt Nikos stand close behind her. A fizz of desire shimmered through her and she turned to him, the view suddenly losing its appeal.

'You won't see much that way.'

His roguish smile melted her heart and she leaned towards him, wrapping her arms around him, almost sighing with pleasure as he lowered his head and kissed her gently. Her love for him was growing, and moments like these gave her hope that the man she'd fallen in love with would find his way back to her and one day love her too.

'If you keep kissing me like that I won't want to see anything,' she said impishly as he pulled her tighter to him. 'Where are we staying? The hotel?'

'I've made other arrangements,' he said, and a wicked glint entered his eyes, making her pulse leap with anticipation.

All week he'd treated her like a princess, showered her with gifts and made love to her in a way that had made her heart melt. But he hadn't said how he felt, or even hinted at it, and she'd kept her love for him tightly locked away, sensing he wouldn't want to hear those words even in the height of passion.

'And what would *they* be?' she teased, and stood on tiptoe to brush her lips over his.

'Patience,' he said, his accent suddenly pronounced, and she knew she was tormenting him as much as he was to her.

He smiled. A lazy, desire-laden smile. And her heart flipped as she smiled back at him, relishing the moment as he kissed her tenderly once more. It was a gentle kiss, but loaded with the promise of so much.

'Nikos!'

His name, called from above, and a flurry of Greek drew her attention. He let her go as she sprang back from him and he laughed—a deep, sexy sound that heated the very core of her, making her wish they were going to wherever he'd made his 'arrangements'. Anywhere they could be alone.

'My grandmother,' Nikos explained, and he called up to the elderly woman standing by a bright blue-painted door that was surrounded by a flush of gorgeous red flowers. He took her hand and climbed the remaining steps towards his grandmother.

Serena held back as he embraced the tiny woman dressed almost completely in black, her grey hair covered by a black scarf tied under her chin. Rapid Greek rushed between them and then the old lady turned to look at Serena.

'Welcome,' she said, in very stilted English, and her lined face was full of kindness and warmth.

Serena stepped forward, about to put out her hand to take the old lady's, but she was pulled into a hug and had no choice but to reciprocate.

As Nikos's grandmother finally let her go the old lady turned to Nikos and spoke in Greek.

'She says you are very beautiful and she wishes she could say more than the few English words she knows.'

Serena blushed and looked from the smiling face of his grandmother to Nikos. His handsome face was relaxed and he was looking much more like the man she'd first met. He looked as if he'd left the worries of the world in Athens—as if here he could be the real Nikos. Hope grew in her heart.

'I hadn't expected her to be able to say anything to me. Tell her I love her home.'

Nikos relayed the message. The old lady nodded her head knowingly and walked through the tall blue door into a courtyard. He turned to Serena as she looked about her, taking in the array of pots filled with flowers in full bloom.

'My grandmother learnt a little English when my mother was here, but hasn't had any use for it since she left.'

Serena knew her eyes must have widened, but couldn't keep the shock from showing or sounding in her voice. 'Your mother was *English*?'

His mouth suddenly set into a hard line, his features becoming chiselled, his eyes glacial blue. 'Half-English. The only thing I have to thank my mother for is her blue eyes.'

Each word he spoke was brittle, but she kept her gaze focused on him. He hardly talked of his mother and had never mentioned that she was half-English. Questions rushed forward, but as she glanced at the wary expression of his grandmother she knew now was not the time.

It had been Nikos's blue eyes, so sexy and passionate, that had snared her heart from the first glance, making her fall in love so fast. She'd wondered whom he'd got them from, but hadn't for one moment thought his mother might be from an English family.

'I didn't know,' she said softly, and turned her attention to the flowers, reaching out to touch the delicate petals of those which climbed up the white courtyard walls—anything other than look at him.

His grandmother spoke and she turned to look at her, wishing she could understand at least *something*. The old lady smiled and gestured them inside.

'Thank you,' she said as she moved from the bright sunlight to the cool shade of her house.

Nikos followed her in and she felt every step he took, the spark of sexual attraction mixing with sympathy for the little boy he'd once been. He placed his hand against her back as they stood in the small but very comfortable little house. Having him next to her, overpowering her so that she could think of nothing else but him, was almost too much, and she glanced about the house in an attempt to distract herself from the heat of his touch.

One end of the house was used as a living room, with an old fireplace that filled one corner. It looked as though it would be bliss to enjoy on cooler evenings. At the other end was a kitchen, basic and very dated, but obviously much loved. The tiny windows in the thick walls let in only a small amount of light, but Serena was thankful to be out of the sun.

'Relax,' Nikos said, his voice deep and sexy as he showed her to the only comfortable-looking chair in the room. 'Lunch is a bit of a tradition when I visit my grandmother.'

He looked down at her as she sat, and again she saw much more of the man she'd fallen in love with. Leaving Athens and his business behind must allow him to relax, to be who he really was. But whoever he was the spark of attraction hadn't diminished.

She sat back, then realised she must be in his grandmother's chair. She was about to get up to offer it to her when the old lady smiled, a twinkle making her eyes sparkle just as Nikos's sometimes did.

'Please—have your chair,' Serena said, frustrated by the language barrier.

'No.' The old lady shook her head and sat on one of the four chairs around the small table, speaking to Nikos, who was now busy in the kitchen.

Serena looked at his broad shoulders as he set about preparing their lunch, his back to both her and his grandmother. Seeing him in this environment, almost without a trace of the ruthless streak he used as his barrier against the world and especially against her, made her heart soften and love flow.

'She says you are the guest and also that you must rest.'

Nikos glanced over his shoulder at her, his eyes sparkling with hidden meaning. 'She *knows*.'

Serena blushed, and the old lady laughed as Nikos returned his attention to preparing their meal. Then she looked earnestly at Serena and spoke, the tone of her voice quite different from the happy way she'd greeted them.

'I'm sorry…' Serena was flustered, not sure how to interpret what was being said.

'She says you hold the key,' Nikos said over his shoulder, without looking round.

Serena frowned. The key to what?

In answer to her thought his grandmother leant towards her in her seat, as if to be sure she had Serena's full attention. She pointed at Nikos, then to her heart, and finally she pointed at Serena.

Serena frowned, unable to decide if what she was being told was good or bad. The old lady spoke the same words again and made the same actions. *You hold the key.* That had been the translation. Serena looked at Nikos. Without thinking she touched her hand to her heart and then slid it down to the small swell of her baby.

Realisation dawned. His grandmother thought the baby was the key to Nikos's heart—but he didn't have one.

She looked at his grandmother, her hand still on her stomach, and the woman smiled a wise and knowing smile, nodding her approval. Serena was relieved that Nikos had been occupied during this exchange. The poor old lady must be longing for a great-grandchild.

'Lunch,' said Nikos as he placed a large bowl of salad with olives and feta cheese in the middle of the table, breaking the moment between Serena and his grandmother, but seemingly oblivious to their silent exchange. 'I hope you are hungry, Serena?'

His grandmother looked at Nikos as he sat at the table

and he spoke to her again, then looked at Serena as she got up from her chair and joined them. The tone he used when he spoke to his grandmother was a complete contrast to the voice of man she'd spent the past week with. Their nights might have been passionate, but by day they sparred with one another as she struggled to hide her true feelings.

'My grandmother is happy for us and she knows you understand.'

He looked at her, his brows raised in question, leaving Serena feeling bemused by the whole exchange.

At least his grandmother was happy about the baby.

The baby she'd been told was the key to Nikos's heart...

The afternoon's visit had been a success, and Nikos had reassured himself that his grandmother was well and happy. He employed local people to look after her, but it still helped to see her himself. She was the only person in his life who'd showed him unconditional love, the only person never to have let him down, and the only person it would ever feel safe for him to love in return.

'We will go now,' he said, aware that Serena was looking tired, and he said the same to his grandmother, sensing Serena watching as they spoke in Greek to say their goodbyes.

'So where are we going?' Serena asked as they made their way back down the steps while the sun began to slide towards the horizon.

'Somewhere we can be alone.'

He put his arm around her, pulling her close. All afternoon he'd watched her, his body aware of every move she made, desire burning inside him. Now he fully intended to take her to his villa and spend a weekend relaxing and losing himself in the pleasure of her body.

'It's just a short drive along the coast.'

His car was waiting, as requested, and soon he was driving away from the village he'd grown up in and towards the open countryside. Its ruggedness always appealed to him and made him feel at home, which was why he'd decided that this was where his child would grow up and he and Serena would live—if she stayed long enough. Once she had the money for her sister there was nothing stopping her from leaving...walking away just as his mother had done.

The villa had always been his private retreat, a place to hide from the world, and it felt as if he was opening himself up to Serena by taking her there, let alone announcing it as her new home. He nudged the nervous vulnerability of that thought to one side and focused instead on the pleasure of a night in his bed with the woman who ignited such an intense passion inside him, unlocking feelings he didn't recognise.

'This is it,' he said, and drove off the road, tyres scrunching on the gravel driveway.

A stifled gasp slipped from her lips as she looked at the villa and he was glad she was seeing it for the first time at dusk. The light illuminated the clean modern lines of the villa, which had been built in keeping with the traditional buildings he'd grown up in. The housekeeper would be long gone and he could finally be alone with her.

'It's beautiful,' she said as she slipped down from the vehicle.

He took her hand and led her towards the door. 'This is where our child will grow up.'

The reality of those words hit him as if he'd been punched in the stomach. The villa he'd built would finally become a home.

A home for *his* family.

His child.

He would never have thought it possible. He had always

been careful to ensure it wouldn't be—except for that one passionate night on the beach with Serena, when common sense and thoughts of contraception had eluded him.

'Not in Athens?' she questioned as she walked into the villa, the sound of her heels echoing from the walls.

'No,' he said firmly.

There was no way his child would grow up anywhere else than on the island of Santorini—he was more certain of that with each passing second. He wanted his child to know all the good things he'd known and so much more—because his child would be wanted, his child would have a father who took the time to be there, to be interested.

'But your business…?' The question lingered in the air as she walked into the spacious living room.

'That is not for you to worry about.' He opened the sliding patio doors to reveal the pool, lit with soft amber lights. 'I have an office here, linked to my Athens office with every technical device possible.'

He intended to spend more time on the island. His grandmother was getting older, and most importantly he wanted to be there for his child. He also wanted to be with Serena—something which had shocked him when he'd first realised it.

Whilst he didn't want to tango with love for a woman, he knew he wanted to try and give his son all he'd never had. He hadn't known the love of a mother but by marrying Serena, offering her that deal, he could ensure history didn't repeat itself. He also hoped that by being there for his baby from the day it was born he could love it as his father should have loved him.

'You and my child will have everything I can give you.'

He saw Serena's expression become doubtful and unease slipped over him. Did she doubt his ability to love his child as much as he did?

CHAPTER TEN

THE REALITY OF her situation began to slide over Serena. Nikos intended her to stay here and bring up their child while he returned to Athens and continued with his life as normal. Was this her payment for the IVF funds? Disappointment crashed over her, destroying the small glimmer of hope she'd glimpsed this afternoon.

The villa was amazing—a gorgeous home—but she didn't want it. Not if the man she loved wouldn't be part of it. She didn't want the ruthless Nikos who'd met her on her return to Santorini. She wanted the man she'd fallen in love with three months ago—the man she'd seen again briefly this afternoon.

He'd shown a gentle side as he'd ensured his grandmother was well, but in such a subtle way that only someone who looked beyond the calculating businessman would see it. As he'd looked at his grandmother Serena had seen real affection. So how could he now be someone different, trying to push her to one side?

'It *is* something for me to worry about,' she said as she sat at the table beside the pool, her strength having ebbed faster than an outgoing tide.

All along she'd fought against the worry of their being forced together, as her parents had been, but after the week she'd spent in Athens she'd hoped her fears were unfounded. Despite his hard deal, all she wanted was for them to be happy together and maybe one day for him to come to love her. Now it appeared he had every intention of sending her to live here while he stayed in Athens. That wasn't going to happen. She might as well be in England, bringing up the baby alone, just as she'd originally planned. At least she'd be close to her sister.

'This is the perfect place to bring up a family.'

His voice startled her and she turned to see him looking out beyond the gardens into the darkness of the night.

'A family?' The question slid from her before she could stop it. He hadn't said a child, but a *family.*

'Yes—a family.'

His expression was set. He'd obviously made up his mind. But that didn't mean she could stay. Not now. His callous insistence that she become his wife in return for funds for Sally rushed back to her. How could she have pushed such emotional blackmail aside? *Because you've fallen deeper in love with him.*

The thought unnerved her and she stood up, restless and on edge.

She glanced at him and for a brief moment their eyes locked. His gaze was fierce with determination, but she knew hers would be soft and gentle, full of concern for her future and love for the man whose child she carried. She wanted to tell him she couldn't stay here alone, a banished wife, while he returned to Athens and continued with his life as if they didn't belong together. But as he walked towards her, his blue eyes darkening with hungry desire, each word dissolved from conscious thought, never making it into spoken words.

'You and the baby are my family now, and you will live here, with every luxury possible yours for the asking.'

He moved towards her, his long legs needing only two

or three strides to cover the distance, but the passionate intent in his eyes left her in no doubt that talking of such matters right now was not on his agenda.

'But what about your grandmother?' She sidestepped the issue as his arms wrapped around her, pulling her close, but what he'd just said had caused an uneasy feeling to settle over her. How could he expect her to live here, in such a beautiful place, when his grandmother had only her small and dated house?

She tried to resist the need to press herself against him, to feel the hardness of his body, determined he wouldn't sway her from her questions with kisses and heady glances. She couldn't let him seduce her again.

He smiled at her, almost hypnotising her with his blue eyes so full of desire and so incredibly sexy. 'My grandmother will be happy that you are living here.'

'But *she* should be living here—in this luxury.'

She couldn't help raising her voice a little. The injustice of the old lady living in such an old-fashioned house while he offered her this fabulous villa was too much. What kind of cold-hearted man was he? How could he build and move into this villa, leaving his grandmother in her little white house overlooking the sea?

'Do you always worry about everyone else?' His voice had deepened to a rough growl, but a trace of humour lingered there too.

Before she could answer his lips were on hers, insistent and powerful. Unable to resist, she gave in to what had been building between them all afternoon and met his kiss head-on with all her desire and love. What she felt for him was becoming too powerful to control, too intense to mask, but she was wary of letting him know. That solid wall, so impenetrable, was still firmly around him, and he showed no intention of letting her in.

She pushed those doubts to the back of her mind and gave herself up to his kisses. With a sigh of contentment she wrapped her arms about his neck, pulling herself ever closer, feeling the rising heat of his desire.

He broke the kiss, his face close to hers, and whispered, 'I love that about you.'

Serena blinked in disbelief. Those first two words had shocked her, and then the final words had slammed into her and what he'd *really* meant had finally registered. He wasn't telling her he loved *her*.

A weak smile played at her lips and an arrow of sorrow penetrated her heart. Would she ever hear real words of love from his lips? Words of love for her?

'It's not right,' she said, and looked about her, searching for anything to change the subject. She came back to his grandmother. 'Your grandmother's house is so *old*.'

He stepped back from her, but kept her hands in his. 'Do you really think I haven't tried to tell her that?'

Softness had entered his eyes, but still her doubts remained. A man who was capable of blackmail as a prelude to marriage was capable of anything.

'Her house is adorable, but so old, and all those steps...' Was he that heartless?

His hands let go of hers, and before she could register what he was doing he'd cupped the back of her head and moved against her, his lips lingering over hers.

'She wouldn't leave her "adorable" little house, as you put it. I built this as a surprise for her, but she is stubborn and she has lived in that house for many years. When she wouldn't leave it I employed young villagers to help her discreetly.'

Serena's heart skipped a little beat. The uneasy suspicion that this was to have been a home for a past lover was quashed. She smiled, looking deep into his blue eyes.

'Maybe you are not as ruthless as you like people to think.'

He frowned at her. 'Don't be fooled, Serena. I am nothing else.' A hard edge had crept into his voice. Was he aware that he'd just dropped his guard, even if only briefly?

The arrow of sorrow slipped deeper into her heart. That was a warning. He'd never love her.

'Have you *ever* loved?' The question inadvertently slipped out, and instantly she wished she could snatch it back.

His brows dropped into an irritated frown, almost hiding his eyes, now an icy blue, from her. 'No.'

His admission hurt. To hear it said aloud, when he kept whatever it was he felt for *her* tightly locked away, forced her eyes shut. She couldn't look at him but she was trapped by his hold, unable to step away physically or emotionally.

His free hand lifted her chin, his fingers warm against her skin, and her eyes snapped open to see his darkened and swirling with passion.

'Don't waste your time looking for love, Serena. Our marriage is only a deal—for the sake of the baby. My heir must be legitimate. Nothing else is important.'

She tried to keep herself focused. She'd gone along with his plans, pushed aside the bitter taste of accepting his offer of money for Sally. She'd believed her love would be enough for both of them. Now she knew for certain it would have to be.

She nodded.

His smile held a hint of relief, as if he'd expected her to demand more from him than he was prepared to give. His thumb caressed her lips and she closed her eyes against the pleasure just that simple touch evoked.

Be brave, Serena. Be brave.

The advice Sally had given her filtered through her

mind like water through limestone and she knew that was all she had left. Her love, her bravery and her sister's happiness.

'Let's just focus on us—on the moment right now.' She whispered the words, desperate not to think too much about the reality of what was happening and unaware that she'd voiced what was in her mind.

He pulled her roughly against him, pressing his lips to hers in a passionate and demanding kiss that she answered with every bit of love she felt for him. If she couldn't say the words she would show her love in other ways. Tonight, at least, she would be brave.

A flourish of husky Greek rushed from him as he broke the kiss. She had no idea what he was saying, but she imagined they were words of love and kissed him deeply, forcing him back a step. His hands skimmed down her body, over her hips to her thighs, making her sigh with pleasure. She pushed her fingers into his thick hair, gripping it tightly as urgency overtook her. Tonight she wanted to lead this erotic dance, to show him how it could be if only he'd let her in.

More Greek words were breathed out against her lips as one hand moved up her body to cup her breast, releasing a jolt of heady desire. She let her head fall back, sighing in pleasure as he kissed her throat. She arched towards him, supported by the strength of his arm, as his thumb and finger teased her nipple. Shockwaves of desire rushed through her.

'I think we should take this inside.'

His husky voice sounded far away as desire rushed around her, more consuming than she'd ever known it.

She lifted her head, bringing her face so close to his that she felt his breath warm on her face and the beat of his heart as it thumped in unison with hers. She couldn't speak, couldn't say a word. She was choked with emotion, so full of the most powerful need of him.

As if sensing this, he swept her from her feet, his strong arms holding her in a firm grasp. Every step he took as he marched purposefully back into the villa shuddered through her, increasing the desire which threatened to consume her completely.

'This is becoming a bit of a habit,' she said, keeping her voice light as they entered the villa and he made his way up the wide staircase into what could only be the master bedroom.

She slid from his hold and stood before him, the urgency of her need for him almost too much. Judging by the hard set of his face and his passion-darkened eyes, he was struggling with the same desire.

The need to show him that she too could be ruthless, could take what she wanted, was rushing over her so strongly she couldn't fight it any longer. She placed her palms on his chest, forcing him back until he had no option but to sit on the end of the bed. His eyebrows shot up as she continued her dominance, her legs astride his as she moved over him, her lips meeting his, demanding, fierce and brave.

His hands gripped her thighs, his fingers digging erotically into her flesh, and she moved against his erection, making him groan. The sound was snatched away by her kiss. She pushed her body forward, forcing him back against the white duvet, teasing him as she held herself above him.

The deep growl of words which rushed out between kisses sounded so passionate, so erotic, and all she wanted was for them to be loving words.

'This is what we have,' she whispered, surprised at how husky her voice had become. 'Passion and pleasure.'

His hands slipped under her dress and up her bare legs. She stilled in anticipation of his touch, and when it came she gasped with shocked pleasure. He stoked the fire of urgency ever higher, despite the barrier of her panties, and she almost fell apart just from that touch.

Quickly she moved away from him, tugging at the fastening of his jeans. His large hands covered hers, stilling their desperate fumbling, and his gaze locked with hers.

'Allow me,' he said sexily, his words so deep and accented they were barely discernible as English.

She slid away as he practically ripped the denim from his legs, throwing his jeans aside without a care. She glanced at the black hipsters that stretched tightly across him and raised her brows.

He laughed—a throaty sound that made a coil of lust unfurl at the very core of her.

'This is a new side to you. I like it.'

Before she could think of a response he pulled them off, lying back against the bed, his eyes daring her to take control again. She didn't need any more invitation. She loved him and she wanted to show him exactly how much—just once, at least.

Without a thought for anything other than this, she sat on him once more, pressing herself intimately against him, feeling his scorching heat against her. But still it wasn't enough. She wanted more—much more.

He reached up to her shoulders and dragged down the straps of her dress and bra in one move, exposing her breasts, her nipples hardened by desire. She arched towards him, sighing in pleasure as he lifted himself up, taking one nipple in his mouth. The sensation was so wild it was all she could do to support herself over him. As his tongue tortured first one nipple, then the other, he moved his hands quickly to her panties, tugging at them until the flimsy material ripped and she could feel his heated flesh against her.

His hands held her hips, keeping her over him. She'd never been in control of the moment. He'd just let her think that and now he was taking charge.

'Nikos…' she gasped as he lifted himself against her, sending a shudder of desire through her.

He dropped down against the bed, watching her intently. Her nipples were hard and damp, after he'd kissed them so passionately, and she moved over him, believing she was back in control. He guided her hips to exactly where he wanted them and thrust hard into her as wild urgency suddenly took them both.

She stifled a cry, causing him to stop for a moment, but she didn't dare open her eyes and look at him. She wanted to believe he loved her so much that he was consumed by the same fierce need that engulfed her.

'Don't stop,' she gasped as she moved against him, feeling his fingers grip her hips as a groan of pleasure left him.

The wildness which exploded within her was so powerful that she moved quickly against him, setting the pace and regaining the control she wanted.

'Serena…' he growled as he rained kisses over every part of her body he could.

She moved frantically, a need so wild pushing her to a dizzying height she'd never been to before. So high she was scared to let go. Each thrust he made into her pushed her higher still.

'Nikos!' she gasped, sitting up on him and throwing her head back. The sensation was so acute she could hardly think as he filled her, moving with her in this new and exciting erotic dance.

The whole world shattered around her and she heard

him shout out. But she had no idea what he said, and nor did she want to know. The sensation of falling to pieces didn't stop and her body shuddered with an ecstasy that overwhelmed her completely.

'Nikos, I love you...'

Nikos wrapped his arms around Serena as she fell against his chest. He couldn't believe he'd been so forceful with her. Each time they'd made love he'd been gentle—cautious, even. But her teasing had pushed him over the edge, driven him wild.

He'd let her think she was in control, that she was leading him, because he'd enjoyed it. But then it had all become too much, and now her heart was pounding so hard he could feel it.

As cooling air slipped over him he wondered if his heart had stopped beating all together. Then the words she'd gasped aloud, full of pleasure, finally registered.

I love you.

He could scarcely breathe, and as if she sensed the change in him she moved to sit on the edge of the bed, her green eyes wide and, if he wasn't mistaken, misting with tears. She didn't say anything else. Instead she waited for him.

A still calmness settled in him, pouring over the passion that had rushed through him moments ago. She couldn't love him. She *mustn't* love him. He didn't want her love. It would only end in disaster.

'I love you, Nikos,' she said again, in a tremulous whisper that pushed him further away than ever.

'Love?'

He was out of bed faster than he'd ever tumbled a woman into it and pulling on his jeans. Her horrified expression should hurt him, or at least make him feel guilty, but it didn't. He had to keep her at a distance—and not just for her sake.

That fact that he didn't feel any guilt proved he was incapable of loving anyone and completely unworthy of love. It backed up everything he'd felt—all the pain and anguish—from the day his mother had left. As a young boy he'd thought he was unlovable, and now, as a man, he certainly was.

'Yes, Nikos, *love.*'

Her voice was firmer now and her chin tilted defiantly as she straightened her dress, pulling the straps up to cover the body which had just given him such pleasure.

'You don't know what love is. You have no idea of its power to destroy, its ability to render a person helpless.'

He crossed the room and turned on the main light, hoping to instil some sense into their conversation—one that he really didn't want to be having.

'That's unfair.' She jumped up from the bed, her anger coming off her in waves.

'Serena, you've grown up in a safe family, experienced the lighter side of love.' That was something he had been denied the day his mother had walked away. His half-English mother. And now he was about to take an English wife. Would she too walk away? Deny her child love as he had been denied? Was that the reason for his doubts and reservations?

'You know *nothing* of my childhood, Nikos.'

She virtually hissed the words at him and he paused for a moment, frowning in concentration, trying to recall just what she had said about her family. The only thing he really knew was that her sister was desperate for a baby. That was the only reason she was here now. To help her sister.

'You're close enough to your sister to know how badly she wants a child, to have accepted my offer of help.'

Anger mixed with confused emotions was making his voice sharp, but she didn't flinch.

'I only said yes to marrying you because I was over-wrought with guilt. I had been accidentally given what Sally most wanted—the baby she'd been trying to conceive for years. How could I live with *that*?'

Those final words knocked the breath from his lungs, making them sting as he tried to take a breath in. Suspicious thoughts hammered into him and he fought the urge to walk away from the hurt and the pain.

'So the only reason you agreed to be my wife was to help your sister?'

'*Yes,*' she replied, in a tone that sounded as if she had no idea of the implications of what she was saying.

She'd never wanted to marry him, for them to bring their child up together. So why had she come to Greece? Why tell him the news personally?

'That was your plan all along, wasn't it?'

It was obvious he was second-best. Damn it, he didn't *want* to be second-best. Not ever again.

'I have no idea what you're talking about, Nikos. I didn't have a plan—except to tell the fisherman I thought you were that he was going to be a father. I didn't expect anything from him—not financially, anyway. But he'd lied.'

'So as soon as you discovered who I was you agreed to my proposal?'

He stood and watched her as she looked at him, her brow furrowing as she saw her future with him and all he could provide possibly slipping away.

'Are you serious?'

'Damn it, Serena, you've made a fool out of me. You've been working out how to get the best from this since we parted the night our child was conceived.'

'I have *not*. How can I have been so stupid? I believed things could work out between us. *You*, Nikos—you blackmailed me into staying, leaving me no option. I couldn't go back and flaunt my pregnancy in front of my sister, knowing I'd given up what is probably her last chance at being a mother. You have forced me into the worst possible situation. But I can't do it any more.'

Before he could form a reply she'd marched from the room. She wouldn't be going anywhere now. It was nearly midnight and she didn't have a clue where she was. Maybe some cooling off time was best—for both of them.

Tomorrow they would draw up a plan for how to continue. They would marry to legitimise the child and he would spend his time between London and Athens if it meant seeing his child grow up. And right now his child was all he cared about.

Serena sat in the darkened living room, the pale glow from the outside lights shining in through the windows the only light. If it had been daytime she would have gone—walked away without a backward glance. She was totally aware that her declaration of love had poured cold water over the desire that had been in every look Nikos had given her, every touch and definitely every kiss.

She had watched him get dressed and known that cold water had turned to icicles.

Now she sat alone and shuddered, despite the warm night air, thinking of that moment again. His ruthless streak was back in play—and it looked permanent.

Behind her she heard movement, but refused to turn and look. Finally Nikos's brooding silence snapped her willpower and she turned, bracing herself for his stormy mood.

'What do you want, Nikos?' She sighed as she spoke,

too weary for an argument, but she had to remain strong—
just for a little while longer. Once she was home she could
let the tears fall.

It hurt that he thought she had used the baby as a bargaining tool to get what she wanted from him when all
along it was he who'd done that. First it had been his lies,
and then his heartless demands for marriage and the
terms attached. He'd known she had no alternative but to
accept—he was that cruel. What had happened to him to
make him like that?

He moved to stand in front of her, his tall and broad
frame blocking the small amount of light and darkening
everything. She looked up at him, saw the hardness he
preferred everyone to see well and truly back on display.

'I want my child, Serena. You should not have come
here expecting to strike a bargain with me. I will not make
a deal for the right to be a father.'

Each word dripped with icy-cold disdain and her heart
sank. All her dreams, every little bit of hope she'd had
that her love would be enough for them both, slipped into
oblivion. There wasn't hope any more…and there certainly
had never been love.

'I found out too late that you were a powerful businessman—one with a ruthless heart—and I wish so hard I'd
known sooner. If I had I would not have come. You lied
from the moment we first met. I thought you were a different person. But he doesn't exist, does he, Nikos? He
was just what you wanted me to see. He was just a way
to seduce me.'

She looked up at him, her gaze meeting the frozen core
of his eyes. She shivered, despite the humid heat of the
night. He'd seduced her, lied to her, and now wanted to
put terms on the life they'd created.

'You are a journalist. What was I supposed to do? Hand

you my life story and stand back and wait for it to be splurged around the globe?'

Arrogance poured from his voice and she looked harder at him, trying to see the man she'd thought she'd fallen in love with. But he was gone.

'A travel writer hardly constitutes a journalist. What are you so afraid of? Why are you hiding away?' She couldn't understand why he was so anxious about the press. Although they had been interested in them in Athens…true. 'A high-powered businessman like you must understand their interest—especially when you've just secured a big deal.'

His eyes narrowed and he inhaled deeply, his furious gaze never leaving hers. 'I am not afraid of anything. I simply prefer to keep my private life private.'

'You mean your mother?' Curiosity piqued, she pushed further than she would have done before. What did she have to lose? Nothing. She was leaving.

'By acknowledging my past I would be bringing my mother back into my life and I have no wish to do that—no matter how hard she tries.'

'Why do you want to shut her out of your life? She is your *mother.*'

'She gave up that right when she walked out.'

The fierceness of his words weren't lost on her, but she had no intention of engaging further in this discussion. All she wanted to do was leave. She'd tried to love him, tried to be what he needed, but she couldn't do it any more.

'I cannot stay here—not like this.' She gestured around her at the luxury of the villa, which must be staffed for him to have had it all lit up and ready for their arrival.

Indignation began to bubble up, bringing all her childhood insecurities with it. She looked at his brooding expression, her gaze locking with his, and wondered how she'd ever thought he was a gentle, loving fisherman.

His blue eyes almost froze, they were so glacial, and his jaw clenched, hardening the contours of his face until he looked as if he'd been chiselled from stone.

'There is one thing we need to get clear. You will not challenge my decisions.'

Each icy word hung in the air, freezing around them, reminding her of the kind of winter morning in England when her breath would linger in a white mist, suspended in the cold air.

Serena blinked hard a few times, trying to focus her gaze and see the real Nikos where he stood now, shrouded in the amber light from his villa's garden. The man she'd fallen in love with three months ago, given her heart and her virginity to, had never existed. Just as the man who'd filled her nights with such passion this past week didn't exist. This cold, ruthless man was the real Nikos.

She couldn't stay here—not just in the villa, or on the island, but in Greece. She would rather go home to England and face her family's disapproval and disappointment at her pregnancy than commit not only herself but her child to a life dominated by him. She hoped Sally would be behind her...that they could find another way to fund more IVF. Nikos couldn't be the only option. He just couldn't be.

She wanted to tell him she was leaving, but the words wouldn't come as he stepped towards her. His handsome face had softened slightly, giving her a tiny glimpse of the man she wanted him to be, and she had to remind herself it was just her imagination.

'You can live in London, if that pleases you, and still have the money you require for your sister. But you *will* become my wife.'

His hand reached out, his fingers stroking her cheek,

and she closed her eyes against the throb of desire which burst to life deep inside her.

'I can't, Nikos.' She opened her eyes as her voice whispered her inner turmoil. 'I can't live like that and I can't marry you.'

To accept those terms wouldn't be brave—it would be foolish. She'd be bringing her child up with the same insecurities and guilt that she'd had. Far better for one parent to raise their baby and love it completely than for it to realise one day that it was responsible for two unhappy lives.

'I don't want my child to be illegitimate. This is my heir.' His hand snapped back and he straightened, towering above her, dominating the very air she breathed.

'Our baby is not something to strike a deal over. I will not marry you, Nikos. I have made a big mistake and I am leaving—right now.'

CHAPTER ELEVEN

A SCORCH OF rage so intense it froze him to the spot hurtled through Nikos. She was leaving. Memories of the disappointment he'd felt as a young boy combined like thick syrup with the anger for his mother that he'd carried for most of his life. He'd loved his mother, just as any boy would, but the total devastation of being abandoned by the one woman who should never have turned her back on him had scarred him deeply. So deeply he'd never intended to commit himself emotionally to anyone.

But Serena had changed things.

The pain that gripped him now as he looked down at Serena was new and far more intense. He fought hard not to feel anything for her. But he couldn't stop whatever change she'd brought about. Already he knew there was a gap in his life just from thinking of her walking away. And it wasn't because she'd take with her his child, deprive him of being a proper father. There was something else too—something he just couldn't accept. Not now she was leaving.

'That is not what you agreed.'

The words were squeezed out between gritted teeth as he stood, rigid with anger, watching as she got up and walked towards him, her face imploring.

'I didn't agree to anything other than going to Athens with you.'

She stopped a little way from him, as if sensing that his anger would burn her as much as it consumed him.

'You wear my ring.'

He still couldn't move. Serena had walked away from him once because of his cold words, and now she was intent on doing it again.

'That doesn't mean anything, Nikos—not when it was given to me as part of the show you were putting on for your business acquaintances at the party. And let's not forget the press. All you wanted to do was avoid gossip and press speculation because of your takeover bid.'

She looked at the ring on her finger. Her hair, which glowed with fire beneath the golden lights, fell like a curtain on either side of her face, cutting him out. Despite the bitter anger which bubbled inside him he wanted to reach out, to push it back and tuck it behind her ear as he'd so often seen her do.

She shook her head and her hair shimmered, then she looked up at him, her expression open and pained. 'You can't even defend that, can you?'

'Why should I have to defend it?'

Something snapped and he finally moved—but not towards her. He marched away, into the open-plan kitchen, before turning to face her.

'Do whatever you have to do, Serena, but remember this. You will *never* keep me from my child.'

Her head shot up, her green eyes so wide and so dark. She flung her hands out in exasperation, palms up. 'You never wanted a child—you admitted that much. If you hadn't lied to me about who you were I would never have come back.'

'What do you mean, you would never have come back?'

'An astute businessman can hold his own, but a fisherman eking out a living is different.' Her eyes were fiercely hot as she glared indignantly at him.

'Is it? A father is a father, no matter what he does.'

'Damn it, Nikos, I came back because I thought you had a right to know—that even if you couldn't or didn't want to be a proper father to my baby you would know you had a child.'

She paused and he waited for the inevitable.

'It's not going to work. I can't live like this, Nikos. I can't do it to my child—not when I know how it feels to be the mistake that forced your parents together.'

The passion in her voice struck a chord in his heart, touching something lying deep and dormant within him. But it also angered him. She'd grown up with *two* parents. How could she stand there and lay the blame on them because she wanted to leave now?

'The mistake?' He heard his voice rise and saw her shoulders stiffen, as if to deflect the word. He wasn't the only one hiding things.

'Yes, the mistake. My sister is eight years older than me, and by the time she started school my parents' marriage was already falling apart. They had even separated—not that they ever told me. Sally and I talked about it as we grew up. *She* became more like a mother to me.'

A pang of guilt plucked at him as he stood taking in this information. 'But your mother didn't leave. She didn't just turn and walk away.'

He couldn't help but make the comparison. At least she'd had a family—the one thing he'd hungered after all his life. His inability to love or be loved had always managed to destroy his chances of getting what he'd wanted. He'd done it again this evening, when he'd brushed aside those dreaded words of love.

'No, she didn't leave. But she made it abundantly clear

that she had only stayed with my father because of me. They had separated, and I was the result—or, as you would say, the *consequence* of an attempt at reconciliation. Because they stayed together, bound in an unhappy marriage, she blamed me for everything that was wrong in her life.'

'Wouldn't she have stayed for your sister too?' He tried to pour rational thought onto Serena's raw words—something he could never do for himself.

'Not when she was old enough to be sent away to school—which she wished they'd do. Instead my parents moved us and tried to make a new start. But it didn't work. It didn't change a thing. My father still saw other women, covering his tracks with ever more elaborate lies, and my mother still resented me—her mistake.'

The comparison didn't go unnoticed. 'And is my baby *your* mistake?'

She glared at him, waves of anger coming from her, and he knew the answer before she even said it. It was exactly as he felt. The baby they'd created that night hadn't been planned, but neither was it a mistake. He was prepared to do anything for it.

He didn't ever want his child to think it was a mistake. His lack of family as a boy made him want to give his child all he'd never had. Which was exactly what he'd intended to do as he'd stood there, anger simmering, the day he'd got that text from Serena.

'Coming back here has been my mistake.'

Who *was* this cold woman? Every last trace of warmth had left her and she stood like an ice queen, strong and determined before him.

'I don't want my child to grow up wearing the label of a mistake. I want it to be happy. But that will never happen because its parents will be constantly arguing. I've seen it all before, Nikos, and I won't do it to our child.'

He saw her hands gripping each other tightly, felt the heated anger of her explanation in every word.

She was right. They couldn't live together—not happily. He'd have to accept that being the part-time father of a happy child was the only and best solution.

'Very well. I shall make arrangements for you to return to England today.'

If she was planning to walk away from him then he'd make the arrangements for her. It would give him back control—make the decision his as much as hers.

She looked momentarily dazed. What had she expected him to do? Beg her to stay? He'd done that with his mother but she hadn't listened. Why should Serena be any different?

He hadn't even been able to call her name after their passionate night on the beach. He'd watched her walk away and despite the way she'd made him feel, the things she'd made him want, had remained steadfastly silent.

'Thank you.'

She pulled the engagement ring from her finger and walked towards the table, which had now been set for breakfast. She placed the ring on the polished wood.

'I have all my belongings with me. I don't need to go back to Athens for anything. If you'll excuse me? I want to shower and change.'

Her big green eyes held his and he saw her lips press together, hinting that she wasn't as strong as she wanted him to think. Then he looked at her dress, rumpled from their passionate tumble on the bed. Had that really happened? It seemed like days—weeks, even—since they'd been at his grandmother's and she'd laughed and smiled. It didn't seem possible that it had only been a short time ago that she was seducing him, tormenting him so wildly with her body.

Those three words, seemingly harmless, had done nothing more than suffocate what they'd shared since returning to Athens. It had all been an act of convenience—one to secure her sister's future along with her child's. She had gone too far when she'd said she loved him. And if that wasn't harsh enough she'd tried to back it up later—as if he would fall for such nonsense. It had been the last straw.

He watched her walk into the bedroom and clenched his hands into tight fists. He would not beg—not even to make arrangements for his child's future. He'd never beg for anything from a woman.

Serena closed the bedroom door, shutting out the black mood that had Nikos in its grip, and sat on the bed, totally shocked that just a short time ago they had been there, making love. Everything had been fine until she'd told him she loved him. She'd tried to be brave, tried to grasp love and hold it, hoping he would be infused by her love for him and help her to create a happy home for the baby. She had been wrong. So very wrong.

With a sigh she got up and slipped out of her dress and headed for the shower. It might be just superficial, but she had to wash Nikos away—scrub him from her skin as well as her mind. She had a baby to think about now, and whatever else happened she was determined her baby would grow up and never for one moment question if it had been a mistake that had altered her life.

Refreshed from the water, and dressed in loose-fitting trousers and a top for travelling, she emerged from the bedroom. Daylight caressed the horizon and Nikos was standing outside by the edge of the pool. Her heart constricted as she looked at him. The rigid set of his shoulders warned her there wouldn't be any last-minute admissions of need, let alone love. Nothing had changed. Nikos didn't need anyone and he certainly didn't want to love anyone.

He turned as if he'd sensed her. 'I have arranged for you to be on the first flight available to London.'

So this was it. It was really goodbye.

He didn't even seem concerned about what would happen once the baby was born, proving she'd been wrong to try and make things work. This past week had been all about control and power. *His* control and power.

'When?' The word was firm and sharp as she held on to her emotions, and if it made her sound cold and heartless then so much the better.

He looked at his watch, the movement snagging her attention. 'A taxi will be here any minute.'

She nodded her acceptance. The sooner they were apart the better.

'Serena…?'

He said her name as a question and turned to look at her just as the engine of the taxi could be heard on the other side of the garden wall.

Her heart pounded so hard she could hardly breathe. She willed him to speak, willed him to tell her to stay, to say that he'd realised he couldn't live without her, that he loved her. She wanted to go to him, to place her hand on his arm, to look into his eyes and whisper, *Yes, Nikos, what is it?*

'Your taxi.' The words cracked from him like shots from a gun. 'My solicitor will write to you about the baby.'

His solicitor? Had they moved to that level already? Well, two could play that game. She pulled her notepad from her bag and scribbled her address down, tore out the page and handed it to him.

For a moment he didn't move, just glared at her. Even the morning chorus of the birds quietened, as if they sensed the seriousness of the moment. Then he took the piece of paper and without looking at it folded it and put it in his pocket.

'Goodbye, Serena.'

She could hardly speak, the lump in her throat was so large, but somehow she managed to push two words out. Two strong words.

'Goodbye, Nikos.'

Every day for two weeks Nikos had sat at his desk trying to work, but that morning it hadn't been figures for his new company that had glared accusingly back at him but tabloid headlines—and they had opened up just about every door he'd hidden his past behind.

He'd kept a low profile since Serena had left. Their engagement had been so public, and he hadn't wanted the humiliation of seeing her absence commented on in the papers. He'd thought back to the brief conversation they'd had about his mother, just as he and Serena had arrived at his grandmother's house, recalling her surprise that she was half-English. Had that really been enough for her to dig a story up? To expose his humiliating past and of course their broken engagement?

As the sun had streamed in through his office windows he'd looked again at the words, and at the photo of a woman he barely remembered—his mother. Intermittently she'd tried to contact him, but he'd always ignored her, preferring to keep her in the past—something he could no longer do.

According to what he'd read, his mother blamed not only herself but his father for his unhappy childhood and she wanted to make amends. And he had a good idea just who'd given her the opportunity to put her words into the hands of the press.

Now, with the sky over London heavy and grey, he sat

in the back of one of the city's black cabs as it negotiated the early-evening traffic. The newspaper he'd looked at this morning in his office was rolled tightly in his hand and anger was making adrenalin flow through him.

Could Serena be responsible?

He recalled the moment she'd left, a vividly played out scene in his mind. She'd been distant and cold to the point of icy, making him wonder if the hot passion they'd shared only a short time before had been nothing more than an act—a smokescreen to hide her true motives behind.

He could still feel the edges of the emerald digging into his palm as he'd crushed her engagement ring in his hand after she'd calmly taken it off, leaving it on the table. It had all been a mistake—that was what she'd said. But he'd been deafened by the thud of his heart as fury had forced it to pump harder.

The taxi stopped and he looked up at the white townhouse nestled in a quiet and affluent street. He'd never given a thought to where she lived, knowing only that he wanted it to be with him in Santorini, but this grand house was not what he'd expected and it only added to the notion that she'd sold his story.

He inhaled burning disappointment. He would have given her all he could. Hadn't he honoured his side of their deal, sending her sister ample funds for further IVF treatment?

'This is it?' he queried of the taxi driver, hoping that it wasn't.

'Yes. This is it.'

Nikos paid the fare and stepped out onto the pavement, still damp from earlier rain. He looked up at the building as the taxi pulled away. He clutched the newspaper tightly in one hand and climbed the steps towards the imposing black door of what must have once been a very majestic home but was now several flats.

Would she let him in? He stood debating what to do. Indecisiveness was a new experience. One he didn't like. He took in a deep breath and let it go, then pressed the buzzer for her flat.

'Hello?'

He hadn't prepared himself for his reaction when he heard her voice, and he certainly hadn't expected her to sound so tired and weary. Concern flooded him, overtaking the rage that had bubbled continuously on the flight from Greece. Surely the woman who'd whispered those words of love wouldn't want to ruin him?

But the doubts that had plagued him constantly, the erosion of his instinct to trust her and his initial reaction to the headlines surfaced once more. They blended with the taste of what might have been, if only she hadn't admitted her feelings to him. But could he believe those words of love she'd murmured at him? He wanted to.

'Serena, we need to talk.'

He had thought they needed to talk about the article, about the way she'd sold his past to the highest bidder. But all that got pushed aside just at hearing her voice as emotions he'd refused to acknowledge tumbled over him. Right at this moment he just needed to see her, to reassure himself she was well.

The door hummed, then clicked, and he pushed it open, disappointed that she hadn't said anything else. Not even an acknowledgement that it was him. Was he so easily dismissed from her life?

He took the stairs two at a time, following the signs for her flat's number. At the top of the stairs he saw her front door ajar, knocked, then walked in, closing it behind him and finding himself in a long hallway. As he walked down it, his shoes tapping on varnished wooden floorboards, she came from a door at the end of the hallway, light haloed around her, forcing him to stop.

The cream jumper and black skirt she wore couldn't disguise the bump of his baby. He hardly registered her frosty reception, unable to take his gaze from her—until he looked into her face. Her green eyes were unfriendly, and glittering like the emerald ring she had given him back.

'I expected correspondence from your solicitor,' she said, her voice firm and decisive. 'I didn't expect you.'

He walked towards her, trying to ignore the dark circles under her eyes and the powerful burst of lust that hurtled through him faster than the plane he had just been on. He had to remember the article—how she'd sold him for her own gains. It was what had prompted him to come here. Or was it?

'I am the father of your child—you can't just write me out of your existence.'

She glanced at the rolled paper he had firmly in his hand, then looked back at him before walking into the room she'd come from without saying a word.

He followed quickly, taking in a spacious room, half given over to a kitchen and dining area and half to a comfortable living space. Large sash windows let in the grey light of the afternoon. Shopping bags littered the floor and partially unpacked baby garments were laid out on the sofa. He looked at them. His child would wear those. Would he ever see it in them? Not if Serena had her way.

He looked back at Serena. She remained resolutely silent, but a blush was creeping over her pale face as she realised what he'd been looking at.

Serena's heart was pounding so hard she almost couldn't breathe, and she certainly couldn't say anything. Nikos looked again at the baby clothes she'd just begun to unpack after a day of shopping with her sister. Sally had been trying to lift her spirits, the whole sorry tale of her last visit to Greece having been splurged out amidst tears as soon as she'd returned from Santorini.

She had been unable to hide the truth of Nikos's deal from Sally, but still reeled at the shock of being told that Nikos had already sent money to her sister, with strict instructions not to tell her. She couldn't believe he'd done that—not after she'd backed out of their deal.

Was he here now to ask for it back? She'd never be able to pay it all—not now Sally had already used a considerable amount.

'I have come about this.' He unrolled the paper and handed it to her.

She took it from him, her fingers brushing his, sending a short-circuit of hot need rushing through her. She ignored it. She couldn't act on that any more. It was too painful.

'It's all in Greek. I have no idea what this is.'

She handed it back to him, still unsure what this was all about, but certain it had nothing to do with visiting or custody rights.

She watched as he walked to the table and smoothed the paper out, his large hands pressing it flat. The signet ring she'd only seen him wear as Nikos the businessman caught the light. She pushed away just how those hands had felt caressing her body and how much pleasure and passion they had evoked. It was too late to think back to those times now.

He straightened and looked at her. 'I told you my mother was half-English and you have come back here and dragged her out into the open and well and truly back into my life.'

'What?'

Of all the things she'd expected or hoped he might say

this was not it. She looked at the image of a woman who could only be Nikos's mother, judging by the blue eyes she'd passed on to her son. She remembered that moment outside his grandmother's house, when he'd told her his mother was half-English. The dismissive way he'd spoken of her suggested that there wasn't an ounce of love between them.

'You calmly walked away from me because you had found something better—my story to sell to the highest bidder.' He stood resolutely with his back to the window, his arms folded and the crumpled newspaper spread out between them on the table. 'You came to Greece looking for whatever you could so that you could return to England and raise my child.'

'That's not true!' She gasped the words at him, shaking her head in denial.

'You said you wanted to tell me face-to-face, that you didn't want anything else from me—but you did.' His accent had deepened and his voice had become gruff with pent-up anger.

She rubbed the pads of her fingers across her eyes, forgetting the make-up she'd applied that morning, for the first time since she'd returned from Greece. She let her hand fall to her stomach. The movement snagged his attention and his expression changed to a glower.

'I'm sorry, Nikos, but you are going to have to explain this. I have no idea what you are referring to.'

She needed to sit. Her legs felt weak and the temptation to pull out a chair was great. But with his dominating presence filling her flat she had to remain standing.

'You were looking for an alternative to marrying me ever since you arrived back on the island. You made up a story about your sister, goading me into making a deal, then accepted my offer of marriage not because you wanted to bring up the child with me but because you didn't have a better option. But as soon as a hint of scandal presented itself as something that would give you a big payout, you left.'

'That's not how it happened at all. How can you *think* such a thing?' She stood and blinked against the anger of his outburst, even knowing that some of it was true.

He pointed to the paper. 'These are *your* words, Serena. *"Nikos and I met several months ago, in Santorini."'*

Involuntarily she moved towards him, sensing the pain behind his anger. He moved to pace across the room like a caged animal and she dragged out a chair, not able to stand any longer.

'I shouldn't have said anything about my sister, but that wasn't the reason I said yes to you.'

'Why *did* you say yes, Serena?' He folded his arms across his chest, looking more territorial by the minute.

What should she say? Should she tell him it was because she'd loved him? No, she couldn't do that—not after his reaction to those words two weeks ago.

'I hoped we could make it work—for the baby's sake. I didn't want to be a single parent, Nikos. And I felt guilty for having what Sally most wanted. All I knew was that I couldn't let my child grow up with the same guilt I had known as a girl.' She heard the passion in her voice, saw his questioning expression, but continued. 'I am obviously not your first choice for mother of your baby, because I'm English, but whatever has happened between you and your mother I have not breathed a word of it to anyone. Why *would* I?'

'Why would you?' He repeated her question and moved towards the table, pulling out the other chair and sitting down.

His knee touched hers and fire leapt within her. 'What could I gain—even if I knew what the story was?'

'A big payment, to start with.'

She gasped in surprise. How could he think that of her? 'You think I've used my contacts to dig this up?' She pushed the paper away from her, hurt at his accusation.

'I told you'd I'd support you—this wasn't needed.'

He placed his hand on the newspaper, the movement bringing him closer to her, and she fought hard not to inhale the heady masculine scent that was Nikos.

'I haven't written this, and I haven't had anything to do with it—but I will use my contacts to prove that if you can't take my word. The only piece I've written that is remotely connected with you is about holidaying in Santorini... about the restaurants and the sights.'

She pointed to the printed copy of her article on her small desk, awaiting a final reading before being submitted. He looked at it, then straight back at her, and she saw his guard slip, saw the pain in his eyes. Pain carried through childhood—the kind she too knew about.

He glared at the newspaper, a deep and heavy scowl on his face. Then realisation hit her hard. She *had* spoken to one person—and said those exact words.

'I *did* say that to someone...' she whispered softly.

He looked at her slowly, disappointment washing over his face. 'Who?'

'At the party—I said that to Christos.'

Suspicion filled her mind. Could *he* be the source of this story?

She put her hand over his as it lay on the paper and, emboldened when he didn't withdraw it, asked quietly, 'What happened, Nikos? Please tell me?'

'As far I am concerned it's in the past—and that's where it should stay.'

He pulled his hand back and she felt the moment being lost—especially when he got up and walked to the window and stood looking out at the street.

She moved quietly and walked over to him, leaning against the other side of the window. His profile was set in firm lines and everything about his stance was defensive.

'I need to know, Nikos. Whoever sold this story, and whatever the outcome for us, that woman is your mother—your child's grandmother.'

He looked at her, and she inhaled deeply as she saw the naked emotions in his eyes.

'When I was six she told me she was going away, that she didn't love my father—or me. She told me I was unlovable.'

Serena's heart filled with pity for the little boy she imagined him as. How could any woman leave her young son? No wonder he'd been so angry, so against fatherhood. She looked deep into his eyes, offering comfort with hers but not saying anything.

Nikos was numb. He didn't see the tall white houses on the opposite side of the street. That image was replaced by the sea and the empty horizon on Santorini as he'd stood and waited each day in the hope that the next boat in to the island would have his mother on it—that she would return saying she'd made a mistake and of course she loved him.

'If my father had loved her more she would never have left.'

He felt Serena touch his arm, her hand warm through his suit jacket, but it wasn't enough to pull him from the past. Even the question of who had exposed the story wasn't important now. All he could see was his mother walking away. All he could feel was the agony of knowing he wasn't loved.

'Sometimes it's better if parents *don't* stay together. Maybe that's what happened with your parents.'

He looked at her, remembering all she'd told him about her childhood. How she felt she was the mistake that had forced her parents to stay together. Was *he* the mistake that had forced his apart?

'I have never seen her since.' The admission made him press his jaw firmly together. It was the first time he'd wanted to talk about her for a very long time. 'I gave up wishing she'd come back for me. Accepted she didn't love me.'

'Nikos...'

She breathed his name and he finally looked at her. Those big green eyes were filling with undisguised tears and he wanted to kiss her, to feel her lips on his, bringing him to life once more with her love. A love he'd rejected. A love he didn't deserve.

He moved away from her—away from temptation—and as he did so saw again the baby clothes neatly laid out on the sofa. Not only did he not deserve Serena's love, he didn't deserve his child's love either.

'I wanted to be a better father to my child.'

He spoke harshly, glad of the anger that filled him as he thought of how cold and distant his own father had been and how Serena's walking away had deprived him of that chance to right the past.

'And you will be—once we sort things out between us. I may not be able to pay you back the money you gave my sister, but I will never stop you seeing your baby grow up, Nikos. It will be difficult, given that I'm here in London and you are in Greece, but we have to make it work.'

He turned and looked at her. The firm tone of her voice brooked no argument. He knew there and then that his being there wasn't serving any purpose. If anything it was making things worse.

She hadn't written that article, or instigated it in any way. Christos had betrayed him, exploiting his weakness for all to see. Deep down he'd known Serena wasn't behind it, but he had used the excuse of confronting her to fly to London. He'd needed to see her, to hear her voice.

He didn't understand this burning need. Lust and passion were involved—and, yes, she was having his baby— but it was more than that. It was so much more than he deserved.

'I want the baby to have my name.'

When she'd left the bedroom after their last night of passion he'd decided that they would have to marry, no matter where they lived, and that still stood. His child must legitimately have his name.

'That can be arranged,' she said with a hint of suspicion in her voice. 'You can be named on the birth certificate as the father.'

'That's not enough,' he said, and found himself moving towards her.

He wanted to touch her, to place his hand over his baby. Then he paused, remembering what his grandmother had said to Serena. He'd been distracted with lunch preparations that day, but he could still hear himself translating what she'd said.

You hold the key.

At the time he'd put it down to the ramblings of an elderly lady, but now he wasn't so sure. *Was* the baby they'd created the key? And, if so, to what? Had she meant the key to being able to lay his ghosts to rest, to being the kind of father he'd wanted to have?

It was then that he knew. His grandmother believed the baby was the key to burying his past—but he could only do that if he married Serena and if they lived as a family. The happy, loving family he'd never had.

'There isn't any other way to do it.'

She looked imploringly at him and her words dragged him back to the present. She was wrong. There was one thing they could do.

'There is if you marry me and return to Greece.'

CHAPTER TWELVE

IT WAS AS if the floor had opened up and swallowed her. To have Nikos in her home was unexpected, but for him to accuse her first of selling his story, then all but demand she go back and marry him, was beyond comprehension. Was this his way of collecting her debt?

For a moment, when he'd spoken of his childhood, she'd almost gone to him, almost put her arms around him and given in to the need to hold him close. But those last words had cooled the burning need.

She'd tried to love him, but he had pushed her away, locked her out. She had wanted them to be a couple, but it hadn't worked. Neither would getting married because of the baby. She was convinced they would be exactly the same as her parents had been. Unhappy.

'No, Nikos. We have already proved that's a bad idea.'

She shook her head in denial as he moved closer to her, looming over her, his height making her feel intimidated, as it had the night she'd first returned to Santorini. He would make a formidable adversary in the boardroom, of that she was sure, but here in her home she wouldn't be dominated.

'Is that so?'

'You know it is.' The answer came out in a strangled whisper as she tried to hold on to her senses, even as the fresh scent of his aftershave invaded every nerve cell in her body.

How had they come so far from that week of romance they'd spent in Athens? The emerald ring he'd given her hadn't changed anything—probably because he hadn't given it out of love, as the assistant had thought. She lowered her gaze, not wanting to look into his, not wanting to see those blue eyes darken and warm with passion. The husky note in his voice was one she'd come to know, one she loved, and one that would spell disaster if she responded now.

He reached for her face, his fingers briefly touching her chin. He wanted her to look up at him. She ducked out of his way and moved into the living room, quickly collecting up the baby clothes she'd bought that afternoon. Those few hours of shopping with Sally seemed as if they had happened weeks ago, but Sally's admission over her secret IVF funds still felt painfully raw.

'Please, Nikos, you should go. There is nothing we can say to one another that hasn't already been said.'

Her heart ached as if it was breaking in two. This was the man she loved completely and utterly, the man whose baby she carried, and yet they couldn't be together. His ideals and expectations meant they'd be a carbon copy of her parents. She couldn't do it—not to herself or the baby. She wanted to be happy and loved.

'I haven't said all I need to,' he said as he walked towards her, his eyes penetrating hers.

She swallowed hard as he towered over her, determined she wasn't going to move away again. It was time to face up to him—and to the fact that he didn't love her.

'You made it clear as I left the villa that you had nothing more to say to me. Now you turn up here and accuse me of selling your story. One I know nothing about.'

'I'm sorry,' he said and her gaze flew to his at this uncharacteristic admission.

'Have you ever had any contact with your mother since?'

Suddenly she had to know the whole story. She had to know *his* story—not the one in the paper that Christos had told. She thought of the words his grandmother had said about her having the key. Had the old lady meant that their baby would be the key to healing his past? Surely *she* hadn't known his mother's story would hit the headlines.

'She tried to contact me when my father died, and several times since, but…' He paused and looked at her, the expression in his eyes far away, wrapped in past hurt.

'But what, Nikos?' she asked, gently touching his face with her hand, feeling the sharpness of stubble that was also out of character.

It tore her apart to see him like this. She'd do anything she could to make it right for him, but agreeing to marry him wouldn't work. Whatever was haunting him needed to be brought out into the open, and it was something she needed to do before she moved on to being a mother.

'I couldn't let her back into my life. She walked out on me when I was a child—a young boy.'

She heard the pain in his words, felt it transferred to her through the fingers that touched his face. A touch he seemed oblivious to.

'She didn't come to your father's funeral?'

The movement was hardly visible, but he shook his head.

'They should never have got married. They didn't belong together. I remember soon after she'd gone my father caught a butterfly, held it tight in his cupped hands, and told me my mother was like a butterfly.'

Serena frowned, not knowing what he was saying, but an image of the brightly coloured creature contained in large manly hands sprang to her mind. 'What did he mean?' she whispered, unsure of the relevance this had.

'He said we had to let it go or it would die.' The stark and matter-of-fact words sounded numb, devoid of any emotion.

Inside her she wept tears for the boy who had been forced to grow up without his mother, but she wondered if that had been what his mother had really wanted. Could a mother *really* walk away from her child so coldly?

Before she could say anything else Nikos continued as if he had never expected her to respond.

'That's the last time I remember my father being a man I looked up to. He began to drink heavily, became someone to avoid at all costs. That's when I went to live with my grandparents. I was eight years old.'

Suddenly he looked down at her, his eyes searching hers, and then his gaze dropped further, to the small white baby vest she held. Tension filled the air and she held her breath as he took it from her, his hands so big and tanned against the little garment. He pressed it against the palm of one hand and she bit hard into her lip and looked at his bent head, at the thick, dark, almost tamed curls she'd plunged her fingers into in the throes of passion. He was making everything so much harder.

'Nikos.' He looked up at her and as his eyes met hers again she took the vest from him. 'Don't do this.'

'Do what?' he said hoarsely.

'Make it harder.' She heard the catch in her voice and moved away from him, dropping the vest onto the pile, unable to deal with the flood of love and despair that ravaged her heart.

'I will not walk away from my son, Serena.' His eyes

glittered with determination and his voice reverberated with outrage. 'I can't.'

'You don't know it will be a boy.' She frowned at his insistence that the baby was a boy.

'No,' he said curtly, the firmness she'd come to expect in his voice back, and then he looked at her.

His defensive wall was in place once more. If only it had stayed down long enough for her to cross—long enough for her to slip through and show him what love could be like.

But that was impossible. He didn't let anyone close. She knew that now.

Nikos fought hard to push down the rampage of emotions holding that tiny scrap of material had unleashed. It weakened him—weakened his resolve.

As he'd left Athens he'd kept telling himself he was only coming to see her about the newspaper article. Now he knew that had never been true. If he was honest, he'd wanted to see Serena, to ask her to reconsider, even as the plane had soared above the blue waters of the sea heading for London.

He hadn't acknowledged it then, but he was now prepared to do and say whatever was needed to win her back. She was the mother of his child and he wanted her in his life.

'I *will* be a father to my child—a full-time father.' He couldn't let his son—or daughter—grow up without him. He wanted to give his child what he'd never had: a family home.

Images of that butterfly all those years ago, as it fluttered its wings and flew away, became vividly clear. Was it the same for Serena? He'd bullied her into agreeing to marriage, exactly as his father had his mother—something he hadn't known of until he'd read the article. He should let her go—but he couldn't.

She shook her head. 'I can't do that, Nikos. I can't risk our baby growing up thinking it is the mistake that keeps us together. I want our child to be happy and loved. *I* want to be happy and loved too.'

He heard the pain in her words and suddenly the puzzle of what his grandmother had meant hit him. The baby *was* the key—but not to his past. It was the key to happiness, and more importantly to love, because he would love his baby unconditionally. His grandmother had known that—but she'd also known, in her wise and old-fashioned way, something he hadn't admitted.

He loved Serena.

Everything slid into place, as if a key was being turned in a rusty old lock, opening a door that had been closed for many years. Finally he could admit what had been there since the day he'd met Serena. It had been there since the first moment he'd looked into her beautiful green eyes.

Love.

'Sometimes you have to take risks in life,' he said softly as he took her hand, his fingers caressing where the emerald ring should be. He wished he'd brought it with him. He wanted to give it back to her, this time with love.

He was taking a risk—a risk he'd never taken since he was six years old. He was going to hold on to what he wanted—fight for it if he had to. He wasn't going to lose her now. Serena was his. They belonged together.

The fury that sprang from her took him by surprise.

'You have done nothing but deceive me since we first met, and now you come here and accuse me of selling stories about you. So give me one good reason why I should believe anything you say.'

He wanted to tell her how he felt, that he loved her, but the words froze on his tongue. The urge to reach for her and take her in his arms was overpowering. He wanted to kiss her and hold her tight, but he deserved her anger, deserved the pain that struck through him at the thought of life without her.

He had lied, concealing his identity not for malicious reasons but because for the first time since he was a teenager he was being liked simply for who he was—not what he had or could give.

'When we first met you were like a breath of fresh air—a woman who was interested in me for me alone. You didn't see the wealth of my business, my success or the way I lived, you just saw *me*.'

Finally he could speak, but he still couldn't tell her what he needed to—the very thing that could change her mind about marrying him. He couldn't believe it was so hard to say the words, but he'd never used them, and the thought of doing so left him emotionally exposed and vulnerable. Love had only ever caused him pain.

'I didn't see any of that because you didn't *let* me—you covered it up. You lied, and that hurts, Nikos.'

Her sharp words felt like an attack, and before he could respond she continued.

'Did I *look* like a journalist—one who would sell your story to the highest bidder? It wasn't as if I introduced myself as such when we first spoke.'

'Damn it, Serena.' He crossed the room and took the paper from her, tossing it savagely onto the table. 'I didn't tell you who I was because there was no need.'

'No. A few weeks of seduction was all you'd ever planned. But then what you'd most dreaded happened. *Consequences.* Something neither of us wanted. A mistake— one that hurts so much.'

Her voice was a mixture of anger and frustration, and he heard the wobble beneath its firmness and guilt slashed at him.

He recalled what she'd said about her childhood, about the guilt she'd carried, and finally understood her reluctance to marry him purely for convenience. He cursed himself for not seeing it sooner. But *would* he have seen it? He'd stubbornly refused to accept what he felt for Serena. He hadn't been able to admit that the aching emptiness inside him when she'd left after the passionate night on the beach was love.

The first moment their eyes had met, as he'd been maintaining his nets, something had happened. Now he knew what it was.

He stood and faced her, vulnerability prickling all over his skin, as if a chill wind had entered the flat. There wasn't the adrenalin rush he experienced in board meetings, or the ecstatic thrill of landing a good catch, there was only complete emotional exposure. Everything he felt was there for her to see in his eyes—if only she looked.

'Serena, our baby will *never* be a mistake. He or she will *not* grow up laden with guilt as you did, watching your parents quarrel with each other. It will grow up with two loving parents.'

She closed her eyes as she stood before him, as if trying to banish the image of the memories his words provoked. Slowly and with tentative fingers he brushed her hair back from her face. He heard her breath catch and knew she was far from immune to him. It lit the torch of hope and he pushed on.

'You know what that's like—I understand now.' He lifted her chin with his thumb and finger, willing her to open her eyes. 'Serena…?'

'That's why marriage just wouldn't work,' she said, in

a firm whisper that echoed with a strength he was far from feeling.

'I know your pain, Serena. I know what it's like to be a child who constantly waits for its parents to realise it exists, to want to be a family. You don't trust me, and for that I'm sorry, but I don't want my child to wonder where I am, why I am never there.'

Her green eyes widened, frantically searching his face, then she shook her head, her shoulders dropping in defeat. 'I'm sorry, Nikos, I can't pass on that guilt to my baby. Surely we can love our child even if we are apart?'

'But we can't love each other if we are apart.'

He let the words fall between them, staggered by the heavy thump of his heart as the silence grew more intense. He saw her swallow hard, saw the movement of the creamy softness of her throat where he'd kissed her so often.

'I've been a fool, Serena, a stubborn fool—and I've hurt you so much. *You* are my butterfly, but I can't let you go.' Inwardly he cursed. Why couldn't he just tell her he loved her instead of dancing around the issue?

'It's too late, Nikos. I tried to love you, hoping it would be enough, but it never will be. You threw my love back at me. Now it's gone.'

Her fingers closed around his, pulling his hand away from her face, and he looked down at his hand, partly covered by her small one. It couldn't be too late—it just couldn't. He wouldn't accept that. Not now he'd finally opened his heart to love—*her* love.

As the panic of losing her raced through him she let go of his hand and walked away towards the front door of her flat. She wanted him to go. He followed her to the door, but knew he couldn't do that until he'd told her. If he didn't say it now he would have no alternative but to walk away and remain silent for ever.

Her fingers reached for the lock, but he took her hand, holding it tightly in both of his, then took a deep breath as confusion raced across her face. Finally he managed to form the words that could change his life, chase the demons of the past away and bring him happiness.

'I love you, Serena.'

Serena heard her breath dragged in as the words she'd longed to hear rushed from his lips. She looked at his face. His blue eyes, usually so vibrant and alive, were subdued, veiled with what looked like pain.

'No...' she whispered, and tried to pull her hand free, but he held it firmly.

How could he expect her to believe him now, when he'd proved he would do anything he had to to get what he wanted? She had to remember the deal he'd so coldly laid before her.

'It's too late.'

'Too late?'

His deep voice rumbled around the narrow hallway, his proximity making her light-headed. Why couldn't he just leave? Then she could crawl into her bed and cry her heart out all night. Tomorrow would be a fresh start, the beginning of her life without Nikos.

'Too late for what?'

'Why have you waited until now to tell me?' She surprised herself with the forthright and businesslike tone of her words and lifted her chin, determined to show a fighting spirit she was far from feeling.

He frowned, and before he could answer she did it for him. 'Because you will do anything to get what you want. You lied to me once, Nikos, I won't fall for it again. I don't love you. I can't love a man with such a ruthless and closed heart.'

'You have changed that, Serena. My grandmother saw it even when I hadn't.' He kept her hand firmly in his and moved towards her, forcing her back against the wall of the hallway. 'She saw what I had been trying to ignore—that I was in love with you.'

She lowered her gaze, refusing to look into his eyes, refusing to be drawn in yet again. 'That doesn't matter—it's still too late. I don't love you.'

Each word was a painful lie. She *did* love him, but she didn't dare admit it now. She couldn't have it tossed back at her again.

'I don't believe you.'

She looked up at him, the firmness of his voice forcing her to look into those gorgeous eyes once more. As she did so he lowered his head and kissed her, the light touch of his lips so teasing and tantalising that despite all her efforts a sigh of pleasure escaped her.

This was what she'd wanted all along. Declarations of love and sweet kisses. But were they for real?

'I love you,' he whispered, and his hands let hers go, holding her face as he kissed her again, so tenderly, so gently, she closed her eyes to the pleasure of it. 'I won't accept that it's too late. I can't. Not when I love you so much. I can't let you go, Serena.'

She pulled away from him, her breath ragged with desire and threatening tears. She leant against the wall, her heart beating rapidly with a confused mix of elation and disbelief. *Did* he love her? Or was he just saying what he thought she needed to hear? Could she take one last risk? Could she be brave just once more?

'Don't you understand?'

He smoothed his thumb over her cheek, releasing a rush of need she had to close her eyes against. As tears threatened she inwardly cursed her emotions, all awry—and not just because of the baby.

'No, I don't, Nikos,' she said, and she looked up at him.

She'd known she loved him before she'd left Santorini the first time. She'd known it as she'd arrived to tell him he was going to be a father. But she didn't know if she could risk her heart once more.

'I couldn't let myself love you. I was afraid.' His voice was a harsh whisper, the effort of saying it aloud all too clear.

She blinked in shock. Nikos? Afraid? How could a man as powerful and in control as him be afraid—of *love*?

Before she could voice her question he answered it for her. 'I watched my mother walk away. It tore me apart. As a young boy I resolved never to put myself in that position again. I chose never to love anyone.'

'You have never loved *anyone*?' Had he been alone all his adult life? Was that why he had an almost endless string of women he dated, never settling with any of them for long?

'Each time I met a woman I would remind myself of how it had felt to watch the one person I loved walk away. I wasn't going to make the same mistake again.'

'And if I'm a mistake…?' She let the question linger even as her hopes rose higher.

'You could never be a mistake,' he said softly, and he reached out and caressed her cheek, smashing down the last of her doubts.

'I don't want to get it wrong, Nikos.'

'Then marry me. Let me spend the rest of my life showing you we belong together.'

His blue eyes were dark and demanding as he looked into hers and she felt her resistance slipping away to nothing.

He loved her. He wanted to marry her. And that would banish not only her childhood pain but his too, because she had never stopped loving him.

Still doubt lingered. 'But what if…?'

She didn't finish the sentence—didn't manage to ask him what would happen if things went wrong between them as they'd already proved they could. He kissed her deeply, setting free the desire for him which still slumbered within her so that she couldn't help but wrap her arms around him, pulling herself close, inhaling his heady scent.

'Don't fight me,' he said, and pulled back from her, his warm breath caressing her lips as his stayed unbearably close. 'I love you, Serena. Please say it's not too late.'

'It's not,' she whispered, unaware she was trembling in his arms. 'I love you, Nikos, and always have.'

His sigh of relief made her smile, lightening the mood. 'You have the key—that's what my grandmother said. Do you remember?'

'Yes,' she said softly, smiling shyly at him. That afternoon was etched in her mind, and she'd been wondering ever since what the old lady had meant.

'You don't have the key, Serena,' he said as he kissed her gently on the lips, making her tremble even more.

'I don't?'

'No. You *are* the key. The key to my heart and to my love.'

EPILOGUE

'I CAN'T BELIEVE Sally is finally coming here to Santorini.' Serena couldn't keep the excitement from her voice as she looked up at Nikos.

He put down the paper he'd been reading whilst sitting in the shade, keeping a watchful eye on his sleeping young son. After satisfying himself that Yannis was still asleep he walked over to her, his sexy laugh sending a spark of pleasure all through her. It intensified when he put his arm around her, pressing his lips gently against her hair.

'It will be our first family occasion here at the villa. A chance for Yannis to meet his cousins.'

Nikos glanced across at their son and Serena's heart filled with love and happiness.

'I just hope her flight was okay…' She couldn't quite keep the anxiety from her voice.

'Sally has twins—and, knowing what it's like to travel with *one* baby, I would imagine flying with two is difficult. I did ensure extra staff were on board to help with the babies.'

'I can never thank you enough for giving her the chance of motherhood, despite the fact that I left.'

'I did it for *you*, Serena, to make you happy—and because I'm a man who honours his promises,' he said gently, looking down at her, his expression filled with love.

She loved how understanding Nikos could be. As soon as Sally had told them she was expecting twins he'd done everything possible to enable them to marry in England, so that Sally didn't have to fly to Greece. His grandmother had been disappointed, but a lavish blessing on the island on their return had soon made amends.

Serena couldn't possibly love him more for everything he'd done—not just for making Sally's wish come true, but her own. She loved everything about him, and often silently thanked Christos for contacting the newspapers when he had, even if it had been with malicious intent. If he had not Nikos might never have confronted his past, nor even come to London.

She wondered again if the headlines created by his mother to tell her own story, bringing Nikos's past so harshly into the open, had been her way of trying to make amends. She'd counteracted the attack Christos had launched and put her life under the microscope of the press, admitting that what she'd told Nikos had been an attempt to stop him looking for her, or waiting and pining.

'You should have invited your mother to the christening.'

She looked at him reproachfully but he shook his head, still not yet able to come to terms with all he'd found out about his parents' marriage.

'It's early days, and we both agreed that a big family celebration wouldn't be the best time for her to meet everyone.'

'I think it *would* be the best time. If christening a baby isn't a day for letting go of the past and moving forward, I don't know what is.'

She smiled at him as he stroked her face, his love for her shining from the blue depths of his eyes.

'I understand that she wants the past forgotten, especially now it's come out just how cruel my father was to her.'

A shadow of regret chased across his face and she knew he was thinking of the revelations about his parents' short marriage.

'You can't punish yourself for ever, Nikos. You were a young boy. How were you to know the truth? Besides, your grandmother wants her back in the family.'

'You and my grandmother are conspiring against me, I see.' A hint of amusement lingered in his voice.

Serena laughed. 'Would I do such a thing?'

'Yes, you would.'

He made a show of annoyance, but Serena was too excited about the arrival of her family for the christening—including her parents, who were, amazingly, travelling together—to let anything spoil it.

'Okay, you get your way. She didn't see our wedding or the blessing, so I *will* ask her to come to the christening.'

'You could both fly back from Athens together after your meeting tomorrow.' She dropped the suggestion lightly as she took a sip of her iced water, pretending not to notice the suspicion narrowing his eyes.

'We could…yes.'

Nikos looked reproachfully at his wife, but she just laughed, and he fought the urge to silence her with a kiss. He thought of the long, painful talks he'd had with his mother, which had revealed that whilst she hadn't wanted to remain married to his father she'd never wanted to leave her son. At first he hadn't been able to understand why she hadn't tried to mend the marriage, but then all the sorry truth had come out and bit by bit he had learned to forgive her.

Now he just needed to let go of the past once and for all. He was married to a woman he adored, and loved with all his heart, and he had the most beautiful son. He had everything he'd thought impossible.

'It would make us complete—the family, I mean,' she said wistfully. 'Grandparents on each side for Yannis, and even a wonderful great-grandmother.'

'I love you, Serena.' He kissed her passionately as she looked up at him. 'And if it makes you happy I will insist she comes.'

'Being with the man I love makes me happy.'

He held her against him, his life complete, and knew he wouldn't change a thing.

* * * * *

#3373 SEDUCING HIS ENEMY'S DAUGHTER
by Annie West
Donato Salazar's plan to jilt his enemy's daughter is the ultimate revenge and beautiful Ella Sanderson is certainly sweet enough! But as their fake wedding day approaches, one question weighs heavily on Donato's mind: to love, honor...and betray?

#3374 HIDDEN IN THE SHEIKH'S HAREM
by Michelle Conder
When Prince Zachim Darkhan escapes capture he takes the daughter of his nemesis with him. But while Farah Hajjar is hidden in his harem the line between hatred and desire soon blurs, leading Zachim past the point of no return.

#3375 THE RETURN OF ANTONIDES
by Anne McAllister
Widow Holly Halloran's fresh start is only a plane ride away, until Lukas Antonides—the man she wishes she could forget—strides arrogantly back into her life. As tension mounts between them, so too does that bubbling attraction of old...

#3376 RESISTING THE SICILIAN PLAYBOY
by Amanda Cinelli
Leo Valente is as notorious as the tabloids say he is. But feisty wedding planner Dara Devlin isn't deterred. She needs his family castle for her top client, so she boldly accepts Leo's outrageous challenge to be his fake girlfriend!

REQUEST YOUR FREE BOOKS!

HARLEQUIN

Presents®

2 FREE NOVELS PLUS
2 FREE GIFTS!

PASSION
GUARANTEED
SEDUCTION

YES! Please send me 2 FREE Harlequin Presents® novels and my 2 FREE gifts (gifts are worth about $10). After receiving them, if I don't wish to receive any more books, I can return the shipping statement marked "cancel." If I don't cancel, I will receive 6 brand-new novels every month and be billed just $4.30 per book in the U.S. or $5.24 per book in Canada. That's a saving of at least 13% off the cover price! It's quite a bargain! Shipping and handling is just 50¢ per book in the U.S. and 75¢ per book in Canada.* I understand that accepting the 2 free books and gifts places me under no obligation to buy anything. I can always return a shipment and cancel at any time. Even if I never buy another book, the two free books and gifts are mine to keep forever.

106/306 HDN GHRP

Name	(PLEASE PRINT)
Address	Apt. #
City	State/Prov.	Zip/Postal Code

Signature (if under 18, a parent or guardian must sign)

Mail to the **Reader Service:**
IN U.S.A.: P.O. Box 1867, Buffalo, NY 14240-1867
IN CANADA: P.O. Box 609, Fort Erie, Ontario L2A 5X3

**Are you a current subscriber to Harlequin Presents® books
and want to receive the larger-print edition?
Call 1-800-873-8635 or visit www.ReaderService.com.**

* Terms and prices subject to change without notice. Prices do not include applicable taxes. Sales tax applicable in N.Y. Canadian residents will be charged applicable taxes. Offer not valid in Quebec. This offer is limited to one order per household. Not valid for current subscribers to Harlequin Presents books. All orders subject to credit approval. Credit or debit balances in a customer's account(s) may be offset by any other outstanding balance owed by or to the customer. Please allow 4 to 6 weeks for delivery. Offer available while quantities last.

Your Privacy—The Reader Service is committed to protecting your privacy. Our Privacy Policy is available online at www.ReaderService.com or upon request from the Reader Service.

We make a portion of our mailing list available to reputable third parties that offer products we believe may interest you. If you prefer that we not exchange your name with third parties, or if you wish to clarify or modify your communication preferences, please visit us at www.ReaderService.com/consumerschoice or write to us at Reader Service Preference Service, P.O. Box 9062, Buffalo, NY 14240-9062. Include your complete name and address.

HP15

"Are you asking me to pose as your date?"

"What other reason would we have for being in Palermo together? I think it's the most believable scenario, don't you?"

Maybe it was tiredness after the past twenty-four hours catching up with her, but Dara felt a wave of hysterical laughter threatening to bubble up to the surface. The thought that anyone would believe a man like Leo Valente was dating a plain Irish nobody like her was absolutely ludicrous.

He continued, oblivious to her stunned reaction. "You would leave the business talk to me. All I'd need is for you to act as a buffer of sorts—play on your history with his family. Someone with a personal connection to smooth the way."

"A buffer? That sounds so flattering…" she muttered.

"You would get all the benefits of being my companion, being a guest at an exclusive event. It would be enjoyable, I believe."

"Umberto Lucchesi is a powerful man. He must have good reason not to trust you," she mused. "I'm not quite sure I can risk my reputation."

"I'm a powerful man, Dara. You climbed up a building to get a meeting with me. I'm offering you an opportunity to get exactly what you want. It's up to you if you take it or not."

The limo came to a stop. Dara looked out at the hotel's dull gray exterior, trying desperately to get a handle on the situation. He was essentially offering her the *castello* on a silver platter. All she had to do was play a part until he got his meeting and she would be done.

"What happens if you're wrong? If having a buffer makes no difference?"

"Let me worry about that. My offer is simple. Come with me to Palermo and I will sign your event contract for the castle."

She thought about the risk of trusting him. He hadn't given her any reason to trust him so far. But what other possible reason could he have for asking her to go with him?

A man like him could have any woman he wanted, so it wasn't simply attraction—she was sure of that.

He obviously wanted in on the Lucchesi deal very badly if it had prompted him to consider her event. His reaction earlier had been a complete contrast, his refusal so clear. It was a risk to lie to a man like Umberto Lucchesi, but on the scale of things it was more of a white lie. And the alternative meant losing the contract. Losing everything she had worked for.

"If I go with you—" she said it quickly, before she could change her mind "—I want a contract for the *castello* up front."

Leo felt triumph course through him as he felt Dara's shift toward accepting his offer. He'd seen the uncertainty on her face, knew the difficult position he was placing her in.

"You don't trust me, Dara?"

"Not even a little bit."

Don't miss
RESISTING THE SICILIAN PLAYBOY
by Amanda Cinelli,
available October 2015 wherever
Harlequin Presents® books and ebooks are sold.

www.Harlequin.com